The Pot Thief Who Studied Escoffier

The Pot Thief Who Studied Escoffier

A Pot Thief Mystery

J. MICHAEL ORENDUFF

OPEN ROAD
INTEGRATED MEDIA
NEW YORK

Cover design by Kathleen Lynch

ISBN 978-1-4804-5881-9

This edition published in 2014 by Open Road Integrated Media, Inc.
345 Hudson Street
New York, NY 10014
www.openroadmedia.com

To Wayne and Elaine Chew
who understand the Santa Fe Restaurant scene
and also happen to be a great uncle and great aunt
to "Jack" and "Jill" — also known as Bram and Saskia.

The Pot Thief
Who Studied
Escoffier

1

The sallow-faced man sauntered into my Old Town pottery shop on a brisk November day and asked to use my restroom.

I directed him to the public ones around the corner.

"You don't have any customers," he said, "so I figured your restroom would be empty."

I didn't appreciate his reminder that business was slow, but I held my tongue.

His need was evidently less than urgent because he started walking around the shop examining the merchandise. "These pots are old, right?"

"Some of them are. The old ones have the estimated date and the culture they represent written on the card in front of them. Most of the ones from the last hundred years or so have the potter's name, the pueblo and the date."

"So some of these potters are alive?"

Strangers wanting to use my bathroom annoy me, but this one

seemed to be transitioning from irritant to customer. I came out from behind the counter and placed a pot in his hand. "The man who made this is alive and well. He does excellent work, and his pots are bargains because he's not yet as famous as he will be."

"How can I contact him?"

"You can't."

His yellowish-brown complexion darkened to a strange ochre. At least the part of it I could see. Most of his face was covered by a beard. From the look of him, I guessed he had grown it to hide a weak chin or a cruel mouth or some other facial feature with a personality disorder.

"I'm not trying to cut you out of a sale," he said. "I want to commission him to make some chargers."

I pictured a herd of ceramic horses. "Chargers?"

"The decorative plates you see when you're seated at a fine restaurant. They are strictly for show and are taken away when the first course arrives. I'm starting a new restaurant and need some special chargers."

Why he was telling me this I couldn't guess. "The potter's name is Seepu," I said. "He does only traditional pottery."

"I'd pay handsomely."

"Wouldn't matter. I pay him several thousand dollars for a small pot, and even at that price he's willing to sell me only two or three a year."

He placed the pot back on the shelf and picked up one from Zuni.

"How about this guy?"

"Mr. . . ."

"Molinero. Santiago Molinero." He stuck his hand out awkwardly and we shook.

"I'm Hubert," I told him, "but people generally call me Hubie. I stock only traditional pottery. There is no chance that any of the artisans represented here will make plates for you."

"Hmm." He walked around the store and selected another pot. "This looks real old. Why doesn't it have a date on it? I thought you said the older pots have estimated dates on them."

It was another of the awkward moments peculiar to people who make forgeries. Or copies, as I prefer to think of them. If someone were to walk into the shop and pay the price on that particular copy, I would take the money, say goodbye to my handiwork and hello to ten thousand dollars. The buyer would think he got a bargain on an Anasazi pot and would enjoy it just as much as the real thing.

But I have scruples. If someone asks whether a pot is genuine, I tell the truth. If they still want it at full price . . . Well, that hasn't happened yet, but a guy can hope. Usually they walk away. Sometimes they bargain. My rule of thumb is that copies should bring fifteen percent of the value of the genuine article. I make a lot of money selling copies, but I make a lot more selling originals that I dig up by the light of the moon.

I'm a pot thief. It's a harsh phrase and undeserved in my opinion, but that's what the Feds call me. Of course these are the same people who brought us bailouts for bankers and cash for clunkers. Or was it cash for bankers and bailouts for clunkers? It amounts to pretty much the same thing either way.

When I was a callow youth, I fancied myself a treasure hunter, someone who discovers ancient artifacts, enriching both our knowledge of the past and my bank account of the present. But professional archaeologists pressured Congress to outlaw treasure hunting, and the Archaeological Resources Protection Act (ARPA) put an end to legal pot digging on public land. You can graze cattle on public land. You can cut down trees for lumber. You can dig for gold or drill for oil. Evidently, you can even drill incompetently and recklessly and fill the entire Gulf of Mexico with crude. But if you take a single pot shard, you're a criminal.

You might be wondering, in light of ARPA, how I can display ancient pottery in my shop. In the first place, it is not illegal to own and sell pots unearthed prior to the passage of ARPA. But since it has now been over two decades since that low point of lawmaking, the "I dug it up when it was legal to do so" excuse becomes less credible with each passing year.

I was in my twenties when I dug up my first pots legally, and I've been digging them illegally for over twenty years. I'm over forty five and should repent, but I know I won't.

It also remains legal to dig on private land so long as it isn't a gravesite, and what sort of ghoul would do that anyway? I know people who have ancient ruins on their land, but none who will allow me to dig there. Mainly because they are turning the stuff up themselves and making a fortune in the process.

So rich land owners can profit from artifacts, but we average taxpayers can't dig on public land we all own. I am devoted to righting this injustice.

Of course I didn't have all these thoughts run through my brain as Molinero stood there with my faux Anasazi in his hand. I hesitated only long enough to ask my conscience whether it would allow me to tell him the pot was original. He was a shifty-looking guy. On top of that, he was insensitive to my lack of customers and wanted to pee in my bathroom. But despite all those flaws, my conscience would not allow an exception.

"That's not a genuine Anasazi," I admitted. "It's a copy I made."

He turned to the light and examined the pot more closely. "Then I'll commission *you* to do the chargers," he announced.

"I'm like the artisans I represent," I responded. "I do only traditional work."

"I need 100 chargers. I'll pay you $250 for each one."

My resolve to do only traditional work softened as I did the math. "How soon do you need them?"

He smiled, and I felt like I had sold out.

"You won't regret this, Mr. Schuze."

The words had scarcely passed his lips when I began to think he was wrong.

2

"The last guy who hired you with a beard got you in big trouble," said Susannah.

"No one ever hired me with a beard," I responded snappily. "I've always been clean shaven."

She sighed. "You know what I mean. In fact, Carl Wilkes got you in *two* fixes."

"Yeah, but he was at least likeable. Molinero seems shifty."

"So why did you agree to work for him?"

"He gave me twenty-five thousand good reasons."

"He paid you in advance?"

I hesitated.

"You just said he was shifty, and you didn't get an advance?" She was shaking her head slowly.

"He was telling me about all these arrangements he's going to make, and it was all sort of overwhelming. I just didn't think to ask about the pay."

"What sort of arrangements?"

"For starters, he wants me to do the work at the restaurant."

"Why?"

"He insists I need to be onsite to capture the essence of the place. He doesn't seem like the psychobabble type, so I suspect the real reason is he wants close oversight. I told him I could work at home and take samples to him, but he was adamant. He's going to arrange my housing and pay all my living expenses, so I gave in."

"You get any of this in writing?"

Susannah is the straightforward type. Once she spots a weakness, she closes in for the kill. I knew she was just trying to protect me, but she seemed to be enjoying it. She's a couple of inches taller than me, a couple of decades younger and a fun friend to have.

I bought some time by signaling to Angie for another round of margaritas. We were at our favorite table at *Dos Hermanas Tortilleria* enjoying our daily cocktail hour. Which sometimes runs more than an hour if Susannah doesn't have a class or a date. Her dating issues are often a topic of our discussions and were again that evening because a new guy was working at *La Placita* where she waits tables during the lunch shift.

"What's his name?"

"Rafael Pacheco, but everyone calls him Ice. He's the new *garde manger* at the restaurant."

The holiday season was approaching, and I knew *La Placita* always has a *crèche* in the lobby.

"I didn't realize they hired someone to guard the manger," I said.

"The *garde manger* doesn't guard anything, Hubert. He's in charge of preparing cold food."

"Isn't restaurant food supposed to be served hot?" I asked, making no acknowledgement of my ignorance of French.

"Salads, aspics, *pâté* and all sorts of things are served cold. That's why they call him Ice."

I didn't think her dating someone known as Ice was a good idea. It sounds like a name for a pimp.

"Where does the term *garde manger* come from?" I asked.

"I think it originally meant the person who oversees the pantry."

"See," I said triumphantly, "he does guard something."

She rolled her eyes and sipped her margarita.

3

I spent a sleepless night trying to calculate how long it would take me to design, throw and glaze a hundred chargers.

Somewhere in my subconscious I knew I was really calculating how long I would have to be in Santa Fe. Not that Santa Fe is a bad place to be. Despite its too precious plaza and too many super-rich Californians, it has many of the things I like about my native state—great food, *piñon*-scented air, traditional adobe architecture and pueblo pottery.

This may tell you more than I want you to know about me, but I suspect the reason I dislike travel is the loss of control. In my residence behind my shop, no jarring surprises await.

The sheets are five-hundred thread count Egyptian long-staple cotton. I know what's in my larder and what I will have for breakfast. As you already know, no strangers use my bathroom.

Being away from home places you at the mercy of others. Who knows about the sheets in hotels? About the food they serve. About the people who clean the toilets.

I awoke hungry, happy that I could do my own breakfast. Secure in the knowledge that a new bottle of Gruet *Blanc de Noir* was in the fridge. I scrambled some eggs with diced jalapeños, tomatoes and cilantro. I dumped the mixture in a bowl, threw three corn tortillas in the hot pan and pushed them around with my fingers until they were heated through. Then I placed them on a plate, spooned the egg mixture and some *pico de gallo* on the tortillas and folded them over. Breakfast tacos and champagne. Heaven.

The doorbell rang just as I lifted the first taco to my lips. I was tempted to ignore it but went to my workshop and peered through the peephole. Then I went to the front door and opened it for Martin Seepu.

"I hope you didn't come to sell me one of your uncle's pots. I don't have enough money to buy one."

He sniffed the air. "I came for breakfast," he announced and walked back to my kitchen table. He sat down in front of the tacos and looked up at me. "These look great. What are you having?"

He sipped coffee while I cooked up a second batch of tacos. When I finally sat down to eat, he said, "Now mine are cold."

I switched plates with him. They were not cold, and they were great with the Gruet which was. Martin stuck to coffee.

I told him about Santiago Molinero. "He wanted to pay your uncle twenty-five thousand to make chargers."

"He won't do plates."

"How do you know a charger is a plate?"

"You probably figured it was a horse. He hire you instead?"

"How'd you guess?"

"None of the Indians you represent would do it."

"Yeah. And like I told you, I need the money."

"How you know he's gonna pay you?"

"That's what Susannah asked me. Why is everyone worried about my pay?"

"Twenty-five thousand is a lot of wampum."

"It is. Unfortunately, he insists I do the work in Santa Fe."

"How long you gonna be there?"

"I spent all night trying to figure that out. I have no idea."

"Want me to take the dog to my place while you gone?"

"How about you stay here? You could take care of Geronimo and watch the store, too."

"Indians don't run trading posts."

I was paired up with Martin when I was a college student and he was a grade school drop-out. The program, run by the University of New Mexico Indigenous Peoples Center, was supposed to give UNM students a chance for public service and the Indigenous Peoples a chance to learn from the White Man. I'm sure that's not the way the Center phrased it, but that's the way it seemed to both me and Martin. Once we agreed on that, we hit it off.

He taught me that his people don't think of themselves as indigenous or as Native Americans. Neither term even makes sense in their worldview. I taught him mathematics for no other reason than it was what I was majoring in at the time. Despite having dropped out of school in the seventh grade, he learned everything I knew about math in a single year.

Martin raises horses and I throw pots, so math is of no practical use to either one of us, but I think it shaped the way we think and gave us a bond. Martin was a taciturn kid. Explaining proofs to me helped him be at ease verbally, something not expected of children in his culture.

"I'll take the dog. You should get Tristan to watch the shop," he suggested. "You pay him anyway. Make him work for it."

4

Needing to walk off the tacos and champagne, I followed Central to High Street and turned south three blocks to Coal. I passed under Interstate 25 and arrived at Tristan's apartment in the jumble of rental houses and apartments just south of the University of New Mexico campus.

Tristan is the grandson of my great aunt Beatrice. I don't know what kinship relation that creates, but I call him my nephew and he calls me Uncle Hubert. He also calls me when he needs money, which explains Martin's snide remark.

Tristan was asleep, the antemeridian being unknown to him. I had acquired a brace of breakfast burritos at Duran Central Pharmacy for use as an alarm clock. I stuck them under his nose after letting myself in with my key, and they worked.

"Duran's?" he asked groggily. The kid has his uncle's nose for food. While Tristan was in the bathroom throwing cold water on his face, I hit the brew button on his coffeemaker.

I told him about Santiago Molinero while he ate, and he responded like everyone else.

"You better get your money in advance."

"That's what Susanna and Martin both said. Do I make Molinero sound that untrustworthy?"

"Molinero may be fine for all I know, but most restaurants fail within the first year."

"Okay, I'll tell him I need the money up front." I thought about it for a minute and said, "I might be relieved if he says no. I could use the money, but I don't feel comfortable with this project."

He had a mouthful of burrito, so he raised his eyebrows by way of asking for an explanation.

"I don't want to relocate to Santa Fe, even short term. I don't know about making pots in a restaurant that's under construction. But my worst fear is I won't be able to come up with a design. I *copy* things. I'm not a creative artist."

"So just chose a great design from your inventory and copy it."

"It's an Austrian restaurant. I don't think they have Anasazi symbols in Vienna."

"Do a goat herder in *lederhosen*," he suggested.

"You're a big help."

He started in on the second burrito with such gusto that I began to think I should have brought three. He has a layer of baby fat, but he's not really overweight. His dark hair hangs in short ringlets, and what the girls call his bedroom eyes are midnight blue.

"If I take the job, I'll need someone to tend the store."

He swallowed the last bite of burrito. "I can do that."

"What about your classes?"

He gave me one his big easy smiles. "Even if I close for a couple of hours a day for classes, Uncle Hubert, I'll still be open more than you are."

He was right, of course. But with my customer demand, what difference does it make how often I'm open? Plus, I might be making big bucks in Santa Fe provided I got paid before the place went bankrupt.

5

Thinking about Santa Fe reminded me of Frank Aquirre teaching us about the 1607 founding of Jamestown. Two ironies came to mind.

First, 1607 was also the year Santa Fe was founded. But that didn't make the history books at Albuquerque High School. I guess they were all published back East. Jamestown was described as the first European settlement in the new world. From which I deduced in the steel trap mind I had in those days that either Spain was not considered part of Europe or Santa Fe was not considered part of the new world.

The second irony was that I had started dating Aguirre's daughter that summer.

The hotel now known as *La Fonda* was also founded in 1607. The rambling stuccoed building on the corner of the Plaza is not the original structure, but it looks like it could be with its ornately carved wood *vigas* and hand-made floor tiles. *La Fonda* (Spanish for 'Inn') has been the meeting place for conquistadores, Indians, priests, cowboys, artists, peddlers and politicians for over four centuries.

As I stood by the registration desk scanning the couches and chairs in the lobby, all those groups and more were represented. The menagerie of eccentrics, posers, tourists, hawkers, Indians, turquoise-bedecked blondes, pony-tailed men, bikers and local Sufis was so oddly diverse that it might have been a caucus at the Democratic National Convention.

The guy I was looking for fit right in. But then who wouldn't in a crowd like that? He wore a white tunic with a stiff collar and harlequin pants with a drawstring. As I neared him, I could read the embroidery on the tunic—*Schnitzel* in bold red letters with *Chef Kuchen* in black script just below.

Kuchen stood up as I approached and towered over my five foot six inches. He had broad shoulders, a square jaw and a crushing handshake.

"Gunter Kuchen," he announced, and I thought I heard the click of heels.

"Hubert Schuze," I muttered as I winced from his grip.

"Ah, *Schuze*. It is German, yes?"

"It is German, no," I answered.

"Yes, of course. You are too short." He waved a long arm around the room. "Everyone in New Mexico is short. Because of the diet, yes?"

"Perhaps," I said, not wanting to argue the point.

"We will have coffee," he said as he strode off towards the French Café that opens onto the lobby.

The coffee and pastries in the French Café are delicious, and it was late enough in the morning that there was actually a table available. I selected a *palmier* and *Herr* Kuchen took a *brioche*.

"The pastries here are good," I opined.

"The ones at *Schnitzel* will be better. I have a *pâtissier*, Machlin Masoot, who knows well the *Viennoiseries*."

I had no idea what that meant. I wasn't even sure what language it was in. Perhaps the Austrian equivalent of Spanglish.

"Why did you seek this meeting," he asked?

"I want to discuss a proposal made to me by Mr. Molinero."

He stuck out his already prominent jaw and said, "In that case, I do not think I can be of assistance to you. Molinero knows nothing of food."

"But he's starting a restaurant."

"No!" he contradicted me sharply. "He starts only the business. I start the restaurant."

"Hmm. Well, the question I have is not a food question, but I'll ask you anyway."

"As you please."

"Molinero wants me to design and create chargers. But my specialty is Native American. I have no idea what design would be appropriate for an Austrian restaurant."

He leaned back in his chair and the sun glinted off his smooth blond hair. "I cannot imagine why Molinero would select you for this task. Santa Fe drowns in local culture. I came to introduce Österreichische Küche."

"I beg your pardon."

"Austrian cuisine," he translated.

"Then you are just the man to suggest a proper design," I said.

"Of course," he agreed. "You must use *Lederhosen*."

6

Susannah drained the last sip from her first margarita. "He actually suggested *lederhosen*?"

"So did Tristan."

"Yeah, but Tristan was kidding. So what did you say to Kuchen? Surely you're not seriously considering *lederhosen*."

I'd arrived back in Albuquerque just in time for the cocktail hour. I was nursing my margarita because the only thing I'd eaten all day was the *palmier*, and the tequila seemed to be coursing directly into my bloodstream.

Susannah idly twirled her empty glass. "Although," she said slowly, "cartoonish *lederhosen* might work for a casual Austrian restaurant."

"They want me to make *chargers*, remember?"

"Oh, right. I guess *Schnitzel* won't have a drive-thru window or golden Alps arches."

"No. *Herr* Kuchen has come to introduce Österreichische Küche."

"Who's he, the chef?"

"No. Kuchen is the chef."

"Yeah, but maybe this Ostrich guy is the *Chef de cuisine*."

"That's different from just a chef?"

"There's a hierarchy, Hubie. The top guy is the *Chef de cuisine*. Then there's a *sous chef*, a *chef de partie* and all sorts of other positions."

"Well, Kuchen is definitely the top guy. I'm sure he wouldn't have it any other way."

"So who's the Ostrich guy?"

"It isn't a guy. I probably said it wrong. It means Austrian cuisine."

"Which consists of what?"

"The only dish I can think of is the name of the restaurant."

"*Schnitzel*. It's a fried pork chop, right?"

"I think it's veal."

"Yuk. Veal should be illegal."

"This from a rancher girl?"

"Yeah, city folks don't know how cute little calves are. It's mean to kill them before they have a chance to grow up."

I decided to change the subject and find out more about her new love interest.

She signaled Angie for a second round and a new bowl of chips because I had hogged all the first ones in the hope they would soak up some of the alcohol.

"In a word," she said, "he's tall, dark and handsome."

"That's more than a word," I snapped.

"Here's another word. He's articulate and charming."

Yeah, and named Ice, I thought to myself. "Maybe his charm is just a front. Freddie was charming at first, too."

"I know, and look how that turned out. I tell you, Hubie, after the string of losers I've dated the last couple of years, I figure I'm due for a good guy."

"The last guy, Chris, was a good guy."

"Yeah, he was. Handsome, too. Unfortunately, he made a pass at *you* rather than me, so I think we can chalk that up as another misadventure in the saga of Susannah's love life. What about you? How are things with Dolly?"

"Good, I guess."

"You guess?"

"Well, we don't see each other all that much. She can't stay the night at my place because she has to be home to take care of her father, and I don't like spending the night at her house because her father's in the next bedroom."

"I know you're a man, Hubert, but there are places to spend time together other than the bedroom."

"Sure, but where's the fun in that?"

She took a playful swing at me from across the table.

I loaded a chip with salsa and ate it. "We do other things— lunch, take Geronimo for walks. I even gave her a lesson in pot making."

"How did she do?"

"She didn't like getting clay between her fingers."

Susannah was silent for a moment, her head canted as if engaged in an internal debate. "Does it bother you that she was married?"

"Not so much as not wanting clay between her fingers."

She laughed.

"In fact," I said, "it doesn't bother me at all. She's forty-two years old. I'd be more worried if she *hadn't* been married. Like maybe something was wrong with her."

"You're even older than forty-two, and you've never been married."

"Yeah, but I'm a man."

"Oink."

"Well, it may not be politically correct, but men are still usually the ones who propose. If a woman has never received a marriage proposal, there's probably a reason. But if a man has never made a proposal, it's because he has chosen not to."

She leaned towards me slightly. "Here's a news flash, Hubert. *Women* decide if and when a man will propose to them. Men are just too stupid to realize they're being led. You guys like to be in control, so we let you think you are."

"I have no illusions about being in control. I have no idea where my relationship with Dolly is going."

"But you like being with her."

"Yeah. She's fun to be with. She likes my cooking. She even liked the *chile verde* popcorn I took to her house on Thursday."

"I assume she invited you to see a film."

"Yeah, *Minority Report*. I hated it."

"That's because you only like old movies."

"The problem with *Minority Report* wasn't its age, it was its premise."

"You didn't like the idea of figuring out that people were going to commit a crime and stopping them in advance?"

"Maybe the idea would have worked better if it didn't depend on three psychics in a big hot tub rolling out a PowerBall thingy with the type of crime and perpetrator written on it. I couldn't believe Dolly liked it."

"Maybe she thinks Tom Cruise is hot. You should be flattered. He's short, handsome and clean-shaven. Just like you."

"Hmm. She did like *Valkyrie*."

She laughed. "Critics called that one the Tom Cruise eye-patch movie. But there was another symbol that bothered me more than the patch."

"The swastika?"

"The edelweiss."

"The little white flower in that corny song from *The Sound of Music*?"

"Art historians are big on iconography, Hubie."

"Okay, I'll bite. What does the edelweiss stand for?"

She pulled a pencil out of her purse and wrote on a napkin. Then she rotated it so I could read it, and it looked like this: *edelweiß*.

"It does look a little less harmless with the weird German thing at the end, but why did it bother you?"

"Because it was on the uniform collars of the Bavarian Mountain Fighters in the Nazi army. The guy Cruise played—von Stauffenberg—was one of them."

"So?"

"Don't you think it's creepy that people who wear a little white flower as a symbol could kill millions of innocent people?"

"But von Stauffenberg was one of the good guys, right? He tried to assassinate Hitler."

"Only after he helped lead the invasion of Poland and did a lot of other really bad things."

"I didn't know that. Anyway, there are probably lots of military symbols that seem strange when you . . . Edelweiss! Of course. Maybe that's what I should put on the chargers."

7

On Friday afternoon, Tristan helped me load my potter's wheel, slab roller and kiln into the Bronco, and I headed to Santa Fe. My supplies were supposed to arrive on Saturday, and I wanted to be there to receive them.

Molinero and I had reached an agreement that I would work at the restaurant to produce a glazed and fired prototype charger. Once he approved it, I would make ninety-nine copies, but we would have them fired at a commercial pottery place called Feats of Clay. The cutesy name didn't bother me. I knew they could handle the firing because it was where I had taken my first lessons. I couldn't fire a hundred plates in my small kiln until well after the restaurant was scheduled to open, which was why Molinero had agreed to using Feats of Clay.

The order was for four hundred pounds of grolleg kaolin, a clay that fires very white and has excellent thermal shock properties. I had it shipped to *Schnitzel* along with some glazing chemicals.

I couldn't get Molinero to pay my fee in advance, but he did agree to pay for the materials. He also charged my hotel room to *Schnitzel's* account and told me I could take all my meals free at the restaurant as the staff were doing.

Molinero had leased a building on *Paseo de Paralta*, not far from the intersection with Canyon Road. The equipment installations had been completed, and they were now in the process of testing everything from the accuracy of oven temperature settings to how best to load the delicate stemware into the commercial dishwashers.

Kuchen demanded that every recipe be prepared multiple times on the new equipment to make sure everyone knew the processes required and to find out if any adjustments needed to be made. The practice cooking produced the food for the staff. Unfortunately, *Schnitzel*—like most *haute cuisine* restaurants—would not be serving breakfast. This resulted in some odd morning meals.

I checked in to *La Fonda* around five and couldn't get my mind off the fact that I was missing the cocktail hour with Susannah. I hung some clothes in the closet and put some others in the chest of drawers. I put my toiletry bag on the shelf next to the lavatory. I opened the window in the bathroom and looked out at the airshaft.

Despite the fact that I knew full well I'd be alone in a hotel room, I had forgotten to bring any reading material. I had read the Bible years ago, and I figured the Gideon version in the nightstand probably contained no new chapters. The only other book had both white and yellow pages. I used it to locate the nearest bookstore.

I walked the three blocks to Collected Works Bookstore on the corner of Galisteo and Water Street. Since I was going to be immersed in a restaurant, I figured I should learn more about them, so I bought *Ma Cuisine* and *Memories of My Life*, both by Auguste Escoffier, the famous chef who devised one of the two systems of organization and process used by restaurants. The other widely used restaurant system was devised by Ray Kroc. They didn't have any books by him.

I entered *Schnitzel* for the first time at nine the next morning, lugging my potter's wheel.

"We have people who do that," shouted Kuchen when he saw me struggling under the weight. He turned to a large black man. "*Schwarze*, please assist Mr. Schuze."

Even though I know almost no German, I winced at that word. But the black guy seemed completely unruffled. He relieved me of the wheel then followed me out to the Bronco and lifted the heavy slab roller with one hand and the even heavier kiln with the other. I followed along behind him carrying the extension cord for the kiln.

"Anything else I can help you with?" he asked. He was unshaven, and dreadlocks flopped from his head in random directions.

I looked around and saw that Kuchen had moved to some other area of the restaurant. "I don't want to stir up trouble," I said, "but do you know what *Schwarze* means?"

"You think I'm ignorant?"

"No. I just, uh —"

"It means black. That's what I am."

"Uh . . ."

He stuck out a huge hand. "M'Lanta Scruggs," he said.

"Mylanta?"

"Not 'Mylanta'. You think my momma name me after a medicine? It's M, apostrophe, capital L, a, n, t, a."

"I'm Hubie Schuze," I said and endured another hand-crushing.

"Like the things on your feet?"

"Yes," I lied.

"And you think I got a funny name," he growled and walked away.

Off to a great start, I thought to myself.

I began setting up my operation in the middle of what would eventually become the private dining area. Someone had put a tarp on the floor to protect it. A work table and chair had been supplied, and there were wheeled shelves along the wall for my supplies and tools. Molinero had evidently seen to my every need.

After a few minutes, Scruggs came by to tell me breakfast was being served. When I entered the main dining room, the staff were seated at a large communal table. Santiago Molinero was standing.

"I would like to introduce Hubert Schuze. Mr. Schuze is the ceramic artist I told you about. He will be making our chargers. His first task is to create a special design. That is why he will be working here in the restaurant. He needs to be inspired by what we are, by what we do. I encourage all of you to talk with him and share your ideas about *Schnitzel*. I want you to consider him a part of the team. If that happens, I know he will create chargers we can all be proud of."

I suppose it was a good speech. I didn't like being called a 'ceramic artist'. It made me sound like a little figurine that sits on the shelf next to the ceramic butcher, the ceramic baker and the ceramic candle stick maker.

All eyes turned to me when Molinero sat down, so I knew I was expected to say something. "I don't like making speeches," I said, "but I love good food, so I'm happy to be here. I look forward to meeting you and learning about the restaurant. I look forward to your help. I look forward to breakfast."

I sat down. There was polite applause. A thin guy with wispy hair stood up and announced that the dish being served was *Gebratener Leberkäse*. Scruggs, who had taken the seat on my right, leaned over and whispered to me, "meatloaf."

I later discovered that *Gebratener Leberkäse* consists of corned beef, bacon and onions ground very fine and baked until it acquires a hard crust. When you first cut into it, you think it's a piece of meat. Then you notice that beneath the crust the texture is artificially uniform. I have a good palate and nose, so I recognized black pepper, paprika and nutmeg as the seasonings. It was tasty but a little heavy for breakfast, even for someone like me who is used to *chorizo*.

After we had eaten, Scruggs insisted on taking my plate and silverware to the kitchen.

"You don't need to do that," I protested.

"You do your job," he said, "and let me do mine."

8

My supplies hadn't arrived, so I took a postprandial stroll around the premises after breakfast.

The front door was so massive you expected a moat in front of it and chains on each side for drawing up a bridge. The door was made from thick vertical planks of dark wood held together with bolts through three wrought iron crosspieces. The extruded bolt heads were cast in the shape of the Austrian coat-of-arms. Austrian flags flew from staffs mounted at a forty-five degree angle on each side of the entrance.

The large foyer was floored in rough stone. On the left, a wooden podium for the *maître d'* matched the front door and was topped with crenellated molding. A bar replete with dark wood and stained glass was to the right.

I had no doubt diners would be impressed upon entering *Schnitzel*. I wondered if they would think the atmosphere justified twenty bucks for a plate of meatloaf.

A set of mullioned French doors separated the foyer from the main dining area which held perhaps twenty tables, some of which were occupied by Kuchen and the staff who were meeting. I tiptoed through so as not to disturb them and entered the kitchen. I had no idea restaurant kitchens are so large. There were four cooking areas with surface burners, ovens and salamanders. There were a dozen smaller work stations evidently intended for chopping, dicing, slicing, kneading, mixing, grinding and generally changing the shape, size and texture of various ingredients.

There was a walk-in cooler and a walk-in freezer on one side of the kitchen and a large storage closet on the other. Next to the storage area was a loading dock.

A door on the back wall of the kitchen led to the scullery where M'Lanta and three Hispanic assistants were washing up the pots and pans used in preparing the breakfast meatloaf and the plates and silverware used in eating it.

Molinero was visible through the window of a small office in the corner between the loading dock and the scullery.

The noise of sliding chairs and murmuring voices came from the dining room. The swinging door on the right flew open and the staff streamed in, taking their stations like sailors on a ship when general quarters is sounded.

The last one through the door was *Chef de Cuisine* Kuchen. The men and women at the stations stood at attention. Not like soldiers exactly—they weren't all in the same stiff stance—but they were still, quiet and staring at their leader.

Kuchen let his eye fall on each person in turn. "Begin," he ordered.

The staff began to mimic cooking activities. Some chopped invisible vegetables. Others stirred empty pots. Some placed imaginary entrées on plates. As some of them finished their tasks, they picked up whatever they had done and began to deliver it to another station. Of course some tasks took longer than others (or maybe some of the staff simply had slower imaginations), so that some people moved about the kitchen and others remained at their stations. As more people joined the parade, I noted they all moved from right to left. Indeed, in one case, a chopper of some sort made his way around the entire kitchen and placed his phantom cargo on a station only six feet from where he started out. I figured out that each person who left a station visually checked the traffic flow. Since it was counterclockwise, they only had to look in one direction before merging.

The Rockettes couldn't have been better choreographed. I stood in mute admiration until the wispy-haired guy who had announced the name of our breakfast backed into a woman carrying a platter of air. She lost her balance and swerved into someone attempting to pass and all three ended up on the floor.

There was no clattering and clanging because all involved were empty-handed. There was, however, a moment of silence louder than clanking platters. Everyone froze and stared at Kuchen.

"*Schwarze*," he yelled. Scruggs appeared in the door of the scullery. "Clean the mess, please."

Scruggs called one of his assistants who came and stood by him holding a large imaginary tray. Scruggs lifted the non-existent spilled items onto the tray and carried it into the scullery. Another assistant returned with a mop—a real one in this case—and pretended to clean up the area.

Everyone remained silent and in place while this went on. When it was over, Kuchen said, "Mr. Mansfield, you are an ox. Ms. Mure, you are little better. Mansfield caused the collision, but you failed to avoid him. You must all be alert for failures among the brigade. There is no point in marching always anti-clockwise if you do not check the flow. The three pillars of the successful kitchen are ingredients, technique and precision."

I had read the night before that Escoffier was responsible for the brigade system used in restaurants. I had thought 'brigade' a strange word choice, but as I looked at the people in the kitchen, it made perfect sense.

No one spoke. The only movement was the narrowing of Ms. Mure's eyes and the reddening of her face.

"Everyone back to the dining room," Kuchen barked.

9

I waited until the first few had filed through the door and tried to blend into the crowd. Once in the dining room, I blended out and went to the private dining room where I began to arrange my knives and tools on the shelves.

At one point I picked up a loop tool, sat down at the wheel and pretended to take a bit of excess clay off the rim of an imaginary pot. My effort lacked the grandeur of the kitchen parade I had just witnessed, but at least no one was going to yell at me.

When the glazing chemicals showed up, I checked the contents against my order slip. There was calcium carbonate, flint, titanium dioxide, barium carbonate, potash, borax and black iron oxide.

After I put the chemicals on the shelf, Scruggs came to tell me lunch was ready. Maybe he should have said *food* was ready—I don't think *Salzburger Nockerln* qualifies as a lunch. Of course I didn't know what it was when Machlin Masoot announced it. I did know who Masoot was because I remembered Kuchen saying, "I have a *pâtissier*, Machlin Masoot, who knows well the *Viennoiseries*." I figured *Salzburger Nockerln* was one of the *Viennoiseries*. Which told me nothing.

When the wispy-haired Mansfield had announced we were having *Gebratener Leberkäse* for breakfast, he said nothing else. That and the way he cowed under Kuchen's rebuke made me suspect he was diffident. Masoot, by comparison, was quite voluble. A rotund fellow with a floppy white toque and a black Van Dyck beard, he seemed to relish being on stage.

"We serve today *Salzburger Nockerln*. The preparation requires eight steps but fewer stations because some stations are used more than once. The steps are measuring and mixing the dry ingredients, separating eggs, whipping the whites, preparing the butter and jam, combining dry and wet, baking and plating. Everyone moved against the clock in an orderly fashion."

He paused for effect and smiled. "Of course in this case we had real ingredients to work with."

There was a bit of nervous laughter. Kuchen looked pleased and proud. Scruggs, who I now grudgingly considered my guide, said to me *sotto voce*, "It's a raisin soufflé."

He was basically correct. I looked it up later in Escoffier's *Ma Cuisine*. *Salzburger Nockerln* is made by combining butter and currant jelly in a soufflé dish. Egg whites, vanilla, sugar and lemon zest are combined and beaten to a froth. Egg yolks are folded into the whites mixture along with a little flour, and the dish is baked to a light gold.

"How do you know all these Austrian dishes?" I asked Scuggs.

"You think cause I'm black, I don't know nothing?"

I was getting a little irritated by his constant scolding. "No, I don't think that. I'm white, and I never heard of this dish."

"You know any black people?"

I smiled. "I know you."

"You don't know me well enough to count me."

"I dated a black woman named Sharice," I said. That was stretching the truth. Sharice and I flirt with each other, and we did have lunch together once, but calling it a date was a reach.

"You think that makes you a great white liberal?"

"You asked me if I knew any black people. Sharice is one I know."

"The only one, I reckon."

"So?"

He stared at me menacingly for a few seconds. Then he said, "I know what's in them dishes because I see it and smell it when I wash them."

10

The clay showed up that afternoon. I told the trucker to drive to the back and I'd open the delivery door for him. It was already open when I got there.

As I approached the opening, I heard voices out on the dock. Something about the tones sounded serious, so I waited inside figuring it was better for the arrival of the truck to break up the conversation than for me to barge in.

Then the voices started nearing me. I ducked into the storage room and heard feet walk by. When I came out, the people attached to those feet were gone. But before I had taken refuge between the canned goods, I heard Mansfield say, "Kuchen should remember that I work with knives."

The trucker used a hand-cart to bring the boxes of clay to the private dining room. I told him to leave them on the floor because I didn't know if I could lift the boxes off the shelves.

I spent the next half hour wondering what I should do about

Mansfield's remark. It was probably just bravado. I didn't think Mansfield was going to stick a butcher knife in Kuchen. But if he did and I hadn't said anything to anybody, I knew I'd feel responsible.

Then I remembered that Molinero had invited me to get to know the staff, so I decided to start with Mansfield.

I found him in the bar studying a loose-leaf notebook. "Mr. Mansfield, I'm Hubie Schuze. Mind if I join you?"

"Not at all. Call me Arliss."

"Thanks. You heard Mr. Molinero say I should get to know the staff, so I thought I'd start with you since you did such a good job with the meatloaf. I know I shouldn't call it that, but I can't pronounce—"

"It *is* meatloaf. Calling it *Gebratener Leberkäse* doesn't make it *haute cuisine*. Anyone who can read can make it as well as I did."

Mansfield's narrow face and long straight nose gave him a patrician look, an image reinforced by his delicate hands and pale skin. He did not look like a man who worked for a living.

"Why did you choose to prepare it?"

He gave me a wan smile. "I am a *chef de partie*, Mr. Schuze. What they call a 'line cook' in a diner. Except in that case there would be an element of honesty. Line cooks do not decide what to prepare."

I decided to interject my own element of honesty. "I take it you do not like cooking here?"

"I despise it."

"Then I suppose I'm not likely to get from you that magical inspiration Mr. Molinero hopes I will find."

He smiled and shook his head.

"Why do you do it?"

"Sadly, I need the money."

I made no comment. He closed the notebook and put it aside. He placed his hands flat against the table. "Ironically, I attended culinary school on a lark. My family travelled a great deal, and I grew up eating in fine restaurants around the world. When I finished college, I thought cooking would be a splendid hobby, so I attended *Cordon Bleu*."

He seemed to drift off in reverie. "And then?" I prompted.

"Then my father died, and my brothers and I discovered why we had lived so well for so many years. He had drained the family fortune. I think he must have known exactly when he would die because it coincided with the bank balance reaching zero. Below zero, actually. He left us with monumental debt."

"Why don't you pursue some other profession?"

"Such as?"

"I don't know. What did you study in college?"

"Classics."

"Ah."

"I thought about teaching, but I'm not cut out for it. Besides, I earn twice what a teacher does. At least I do when I get paid."

I raised my eyebrows, and he said, "I worked at Café Alsace in Albuquerque," as if that explained it.

"I've never heard of it."

"I'm not surprised. It was open less than three months, and both my checks bounced. The only position I could find was at an Applebee's. I was happy to work for an employer who actually paid me, although franchises don't pay much. So I was delighted to get this position. I'll be even happier when the first check arrives."

"You don't get paid until the place opens?"

"We get a small stipend paid in arrears. Then the salary goes up when customer cash starts flowing." He looked at me and smiled. "I apologize, Mr. Schuze. It was in poor taste to subject you to my tawdry pecuniary history. I do hope you will forgive me. And I wish you the best in finding your inspiration."

Thus dismissed, I thanked him for his time and retreated to my lair in the private dining room. I couldn't help comparing Mansfield to Escoffier who had wanted to be a sculptor but was forced instead to apprentice in his uncle's restaurant. Escoffier did not want to be a chef. But when forced to become one, he found both prosperity and happiness. Mansfield, who *did* want to be a chef, found neither.

Mansfield hardly seemed the type to knife anyone. For all I knew, Kuchen had tried to reassign Mansfield to desserts, and his remark that "Kuchen should remember that I work with knives" was merely a way of saying he did entrées, not pastries.

I decided not to worry about it.

11

When dinner was called, I dallied for a few minutes in order to be the last person in. I deliberately took a seat at the opposite end from Scruggs, whose antics were getting under my skin.

Kuchen said, "Mr. Barry Stiles, *garde manger*, has prepared *Liptauer*."

I couldn't resist. I looked across the huge table at Scruggs. He silently mouthed the English name of the dish. Not being skilled at lip reading, I thought he said "cheese dip."

Turns out that's what it was, although fancier than the ones sold on the grocery store aisle next to the *Fritos*.

I didn't bother looking this one up because I figured out most of the ingredients when Kuchen reviewed the offering for us after we had eaten it.

"Mr. Stiles has demonstrated why even the simple tasks performed by the *garde manger* require skill. The quark was not allowed to come to room temperature before the mixing commenced, resulting in incorrect texture. The capers had not been thoroughly drained. The vinegar was obvious. He used too much paprika. It should be subtle, not overpowering." He turned to face Stiles. "Perhaps you lack the palate for your position."

Stiles threw his toque on the table and stalked out of the room. Kuchen smiled. "Evidently, he lacks also the proper temperament. We will cease the training early today. Rest well. Tomorrow will be another demanding day."

"Tomorrow is the Sabbath," said Scruggs.

"Then I advise you to think of the scullery as your temple."

I had no intention of working the next day. I was anxious to get back to Old Town since Susannah had agreed to meet me at *Dos Hermanas* even though it was a Saturday and she had a date with Ice that evening.

Unfortunately, Stiles caught me just as I was leaving. He was a high-strung kid with brown hair and hazel eyes.

There was fire in those eyes. "I need to talk to you."

"I'm in a bit of a hur—"

"I've got the perfect symbol for your plate—a swastika!"

"I'm sorry Kuchen spoke to you like that, but it really reflects on him, not you."

"He wasn't made to look the fool in front of everyone."

"Neither were you," I said, trying to calm him down. He was on the verge of an emotional meltdown. "Kuchen was the one who was rude and obnoxious. You showed great restraint in not replying."

"I'll reply all right. I'll get the bastard fired."

I didn't think the *garde manger* could get the *chef de cuisine* fired, and even trying seemed like a bad idea. "Don't do anything rash."

"I can do it. I know something no one else here knows." He gave me a fiendish smile and stomped out.

12

Susannah's brown eyes were even larger than normal. "M'Lanta? No wonder he's a potscrubber."

"Some people might call that a racist remark."

"It has nothing to do with race, Hubie. It has to do with *names*. You know any important and successful people named D'onoriffe or Shaquillian?"

"How about Barack?"

"That's different. Barack is a traditional Kenyan name. And his father was an immigrant, so it's not surprising he used a name from his home country. It's like my grandfather. His first name was Gutxiarkaitz."

"Huh?"

"It means 'little rock' in Basque."

"How do you spell it?"

"Just like it sounds."

"The Obama girls are Sasha and Malia," I noted. "Are those traditional names?"

"Sure. Sasha is the Slavic version of Alexandra, and Malia is the Hawaiian version of Maria. But the important thing is they aren't made-up names with no history."

"Why do you know so much about names?"

"Because my mother has a baby name book and discusses it with me every time I go home. Just after she shows me the catalog of wedding dresses," she said despondently.

"Sorry."

"It's not like I'm not trying. I'd love to get married and have children, but I can't seem to find the right man."

I took a bite of a crispy chip with snappy salsa.

"What about you, Hubie?"

"I can't find the right man either, although Chris was definitely interested."

She threw a chip at me, but I managed to dodge it. Chris was the guy she had been interested in until he made a pass at me.

I washed the snack down with the last of my margarita before musing, "I wonder if I'm marriage material. After all of these years living alone . . ." I didn't finish the sentence because I didn't know what to say.

"Can I get you two a refill?" asked Angie.

I did know what to say to that. I looked up at Angie's bright smile and said, "Absolutely." Then I said to Susannah, "I don't know if I can survive for weeks away from this place. I almost didn't make it through one day."

"You didn't tell me what you did."

"I spent most of my time conversing with the misfits on the staff trying to find inspiration."

"And did you?"

"Yeah," I said. "I'm inspired not to work in a restaurant." I wish I hadn't said it. It may have jinxed me.

After Angie brought our drinks, Susannah said, "I'd like to hear about the misfits at *Schnitzel.* I love restaurant gossip."

"Well, it starts at the top. I get the impression no one respects Molinero because he's not a food guy."

"It's always like that, Hubie. It's that 'resent the people you need' thing. Every restaurant needs a Molinero, the money guy. Like producers for films. Director and actors don't like producers because they aren't artists, but you couldn't do a movie without a producer."

"Why couldn't Kuchen start the restaurant?"

"He probably doesn't have the money it would take. We're talking millions for a place like *Schnitzel.* And even if he did have it, he wouldn't be crazy enough to risk it in a business that's likely to fail."

"So he has to find a rich guy like Molinero who *is* crazy enough to do that?"

"No. Molinero doesn't put up the money himself. He puts together a syndicate of investors."

"How do you find investors for a business that's likely to fail?"

She shrugged. "People invest in films because they like to think they're in show business. Maybe some people think owning a restaurant is glamorous."

"I'd like to own *Dos Hermanas*, but not for the glamour. I'd just sit here all day and sip margaritas."

"No you wouldn't. What you'd do is work your butt off."

"I'm beginning to realize that. Kuchen is a real slave driver. Everyone hates him."

Susannah looked over my shoulder. "Ice is here."

For a moment I thought Angie had brought more cubes for our

drinks. He was a tall guy with close-cropped hair and a somewhat blocky nose, but handsome in an odd way. He approached at a relaxed pace and said, "You must be Hubie."

I acknowledged as much and we shook hands.

Susannah said, "Hubie was just telling me that everyone at *Schnitzel* seems to hate the *Chef de cuisine*."

"I'm not surprised," he said, looking at me as he sat down. "Head chefs are notoriously unpopular with their staffs. Most of them have enormous egos and function like dictators."

Susannah said, "That's because they're men. It's beginning to change thanks to more women being in top positions."

"Women can't have enormous egos and function like dictators?" I asked.

"Name one."

"Marie Antoinette, Leona Helmsley, Joan Crawford, Imelda Marcos—want me to go on?"

Ice laughed.

Susannah said, "None of those are chefs, Hubie. Are there any women working at *Schnitzel*?"

"The *chef de partie* is a woman named Helen Mure. I haven't met her yet, but judging from her countenance, I wouldn't be surprised if she has an enormous ego and functions like a dictator."

"There must be other line chefs," Ice said.

"Only one other so far. He's a sad case. He came from a wealthy family and went to cooking school because he thought it would be a nice hobby."

"Which school?" asked Susannah.

"*Cordon Bleu* in Paris."

"That's not a 'cooking school'. That's *l'école culinaire*."

"Yeah, that's probably what he called it when he was there on a lark. But when he had to get a job in the real world, it was just a cooking school."

"Why would a rich guy need a job?" she asked.

"His father frittered away the family fortune. Then when Mansfield went to work for a new place here in Albuquerque, he didn't get paid."

"Mansfield?" asked Ice. "Arliss Mansfield?"

"You know him?"

"Yeah. I was the *garde manger* at Café Alsace, and he was one of the line chefs. Of course I didn't get to know him well because the place closed not long after it opened."

"Which eventually led Ice to *La Placita*," Susannah said with a silly smile on her face.

I asked Rafael how he liked working at *La Placita*. I had decided I wasn't going to call anyone *Ice*.

"A Mexican food restaurant isn't a great place for a *garde manger*," he answered. "You don't have the variety of cold appetizers served in a continental restaurant." He smiled and stuck a chip in the salsa. "I mean, what kind of a career is it making salsa and *guacamole* every day?"

I kind of liked the guy in spite of his nickname. "Maybe you should become the *garde manger* at *Schnitzel*," I said.

"Are they looking for one?"

"No, but I suspect they will be soon."

"Why?"

"Because Kuchen just humiliated the current guy, Barry Stiles."

"I know him, too. He was the *aboyeur* at Alsace."

Aboyeur, garde manger, chef de partie. I suspected Escoffier was responsible for restaurant people speaking in tongues.

"What's an *aboyeur*?" I asked.

"Basically a messenger. He takes the orders from the wait staff and relays them to the appropriate station. Sometimes he'll do a few minors tasks like chopping or taking things out of an oven. I'm not surprised Barry isn't a good *garde manger*. He wasn't even a good *aboyeur*." He hesitated for a moment in thought. "Arliss and Barry. Hard to believe. I wonder how many other refugees from Café Alsace are at *Schnitzel*. Some of the names I remember are Terry Schroeder, a line cook; Jim Miller, the manager; Armando Dominguez, the grill master; Hank Schneider, the baker; and Wallace Voile."

"The only name I recognize from the list Molinero gave me is Wallace Voile," I said. "He's the *maître d'*, but I haven't met him yet."

Rafael smiled and gave me a pat on the shoulder. "The reason you haven't met him yet is he's a she. And her title would be *maîtresse d'*."

"Wouldn't it be easier if you used English words?"

"Actually, Spanish would be even better. Almost all the kitchen staff are Hispanic these days and many of them don't speak English. I guess that lets you out of KP, Hubie."

"He speaks fluent Spanish," Susannah said.

So of course Rafael had to switch to Spanish, and after a few sentences between us, Susannah raised her hand in protest to change both the language and the subject.

"A woman named Wallis. I love the story of Wallis Simpson. It's my favorite romance."

"This one spells her name W-a-l-l-a-c-e like a man. But she sure doesn't look like one," Rafael said with a leer.

I could tell Susannah was fighting back a frown.

I didn't want to mention Barry's remark to me that he would get revenge on Kuchen by getting him fired. I also failed to bring up Arliss saying "I work with knifes" after Kuchen scolded him. Wallace might be a beauty for all I knew, but even with that enticement, I couldn't very well expect Rafael to want the *garde manger* position at *Schnitzel* if he thought the staff might be homicidal.

And I did want him to have it, although I can't imagine why. I had just met the guy.

13

I awoke Sunday morning happy to be in my own bed and think-ing about Dolly whom I hoped would be sharing it with me that evening.

Then I thought about *les misérables* working at *Schnitzel* that day. My association with an *haute cuisine* restaurant had me using the few French phrases I knew even though I wasn't trying to do so.

My mind eventually turned to breakfast. My tradition is to eat on Sunday mornings the sort of breakfast I cannot eat every day without damage to my waistline. 140 pounds is not exactly svelte on a 5'6" frame, but I manage to maintain both my weight and my 32-inch waist by walking almost everywhere I go and by enjoying chorizo breakfast tacos only once a week.

I slice the skins of the little devils and squeeze the contents into a frying pan over a medium flame. As the sausage begins to heat, it releases a fragrant orange liquid—pork fat and spices, no doubt—but I like to think of it as flavored cooking oil. Perfect for scrambling the eggs. Then throw in some jalapeños, diced potatoes and onions and stir until the ingredients have become close and warm friends. Put the mixture between folded tacos, garnish with fresh cilantro, and you have breakfast fit for a *rey*.

And a lot better than *Gebratener Leberkäse*.

Which started me thinking about the whole idea of *haute cuisine*. *Coquille Saint-Jacques* sounds like *haute cuisine*, but it's just scallops and mushrooms in a cream sauce. If the scallops are rubbery and the cream sauce gummy, it's awful. Calling it *Coquille Saint-Jacques* can't disguise the taste.

Breakfast tacos sound like something you'd get from a drive-thru or a sidewalk cart, but when they're prepared properly with fresh ingredients, they are just as delicious as *Coquille Saint-Jacques*. Even moreso in Albuquerque because you can't get fresh scallops here.

Unfortunately, my meditation on food delayed my cooking so that when Miss Gladys showed up with one of her infamous casseroles, I couldn't use the 'I just ate' excuse.

"I swear people will think I'm a heathen, Hubert, but I just don't enjoy church like I did when Guy was alive. Of course I still go to most of the Wednesday covered-dish suppers. Do you think that counts?"

"Some people get worked up debating whether you should go on Friday, Saturday or Sunday. My guess is God doesn't care what day you choose."

Her pale blue eyes sparkled as she laughed. "Marsha Wilkes would take issue with you on that. She was one of those Seventh Day Adventists, but she surely could cook. This is her famous breakfast casserole." Her voice dropped to a conspiratorial whisper. "She made it with meat made out of soybeans. Can you believe that?"

Gladys Claiborne runs a gift shop two doors west of me in the same building. She and her shop are as much a part of Old Town as the Gazebo and the Church even though she's a Texan. Her husband left her well-off when he died, and I think the shop is more a hobby than a source of income. Which allows her to spend more time cooking than selling embroidered tea cozies and crocheted chili peppers.

Gladys views me as a man who doesn't have a wife to cook for him, so I'm a frequent recipient of her chafing dish largesse. Many of Gladys' dishes are named after women she knew in East Texas who either invented or frequently served them.

This one started with stale bread. The bread was covered with crumbled cooked sausage—the real stuff—and a layer of shredded cheddar. Eggs and cream were mixed together and poured over the mixture. Refrigerate overnight and bake in the morning.

It was relatively healthy by Miss Gladys' standards, having no canned soups with their high salt content. And it was 'toothsome' as she might say. I found myself thinking that substituting chorizo for the Jimmy Dean and replacing the cheese with *chile verde* might make a great dish because I could prepare it in advance.

Being around Miss Gladys tends to disorient me.

14

"Do you think my boobs are too big?"

It was a question that had never before been put to me. Dolly is a somewhat plump woman, and all her body parts share a common scale. Her breasts would probably look too large on the typical Asian woman and too small on the typical Amazon. I didn't think that was the answer she was fishing for, so I said, "I think everything about you is just right."

She leaned over and kissed me. I took that to mean my answer was good. I was in my bed in post-conjugal bliss. Dolly was putting on her clothes. I like her birthday suit and hated to see her cover it up, but it is probably not the appropriate outfit for driving an automobile.

Her best feature is not her breasts, which may be a tad too large, but who's complaining? Her best feature is her remarkable skin, an amazing elastic expanse completely free of freckles, wrinkles, blemishes and scars. If you took a picture of Dolly naked in a big crib and had nothing to indicate the scale, you might think she was a newborn so smooth is her skin. Of course if she were on her back, the boobs would probably give it away.

After watching her dress, I forced myself to do the same. "Would you like anything before you go?"

"How about a little Gruet?" she suggested. An excellent suggestion it was.

Gruet offers a Grande Reserve, a Grand Rose, a *Blanc de Blancs*, an Extra Dry, a *Brut*, a *Demi Sec*, a *Sauvage* and a *Blanc de Noirs*. They are all excellent. But I sometimes worry that they may be offering too many varieties and will run short of grapes to make enough *Blanc de Noir*, the house champagne at *Chez Schuze*.

The annual December 31 issue of the *Albuquerque Journal* carries a list of the most important events of the year. In 1983, that list included the election of Margaret Thatcher, a person who defied Susannah's stereotype of women not being dictatorial.

But in my view, the most important event in 1983 was a family vacation—the Gruet family of Bethon, France came to New Mexico.

I assume they enjoyed their holidays—most visitors to the Land of Enchantment do. But in addition to vacation events, they also discovered inexpensive high-altitude land with sandy soil where the temperature at night drops over thirty degrees, perfect for cooling the grapes and slowing their maturation process. Perfect for making champagne.

The vineyards are located along what the *conquistadores* called the *Jornada del Muerto*, which you can probably translate even if you don't speak Spanish. It was a ninety-mile stretch of the *Camino Real* feared by early Spanish travelers because of the lack of water.

Draft animals and people often died of thirst. Others were killed by Apaches.

Today you can drive to the area in an air-conditioned car on a paved road that leads to Ted Turner's Armendaris Ranch where you can see grazing buffalo, antelope and oryx. The buffalo and antelope are native. The oryx are immigrants, presumably not by choice. I don't know if people eat oryx . . . oryxes? oryxi? But it is a handy word if you like crossword puzzles.

We took our champagne in my patio. Geronimo was with Martin, so we didn't have to worry about him trying to lick the flutes. He loves Gruet as much as I do.

"I wish I could stay," she said.

"You can."

She smiled. She has a small pursed mouth with ample lips on which she wears clear gloss. "I need to be home just in case. And I'm not sure we could sleep together in a single bed," she added coyly.

"It accommodated us well enough this evening."

She smiled even more broadly. "What we did this evening required us to be as close together as possible."

"Even closer," I said.

She giggled. "Sleeping might require more space. Or maybe you could get a larger bed."

"Maybe I could."

She raised her eyebrows. "Or maybe you'd prefer a second single?"

"Why another single?"

"My first husband wanted two singles. He said he was too light a sleeper to get a restful night with another person in the bed."

The phrase 'first husband' jingled in my head like a coin dropping in a vending machine.

"I'm a very sound sleeper," I said.

She lifted her glass and I clinked my flute against hers.

After we drained the last of our glasses, she took my hand and tugged me close. "I can stay a little longer if you like."

"I like," I replied.

I slept very soundly after she left.

15

I didn't awake until ten Monday morning, too late to fix breakfast. So after showering and dressing, I drove to the nearest Blake's and bought a #7, their breakfast burrito with *chorizo*, potatoes, onions and *chile verde*.

I ate the burrito on the way to Santa Fe and arrived at *Schnitzel* just as lunch was being served. It was *Schokogugelhupf*, which I learned later was a sort of chocolate Bundt cake. I could have burned off the calories from its chocolate, butter and golden icing sugar simply by trying to pronounce it, but it didn't seem a fitting dessert for a Blake's burrito, so I went to my work area.

I mixed a simple slurry using thirty units each of the grolleg, calcium carbonate and barium carbonate, ten units of flint, four of titanium dioxide and a small amount of water to get the consistency right. I was planning to do a test firing to see how the glaze looked on the clay.

I was busy placing the chemicals back on the shelf and mentally noting how much of each I had used when Alain Billot, the *sous chef*, came to see me.

Billot's pointed chin and aquiline nose gave him a cubist look. His light brown hair was tousled, his eyes clear and bright.

"I have come for the interview Mr. Molinero wants me to have with you," he said rather stiffly in a French accent, his arms folded behind his back. Then he smiled and brought his hands to his front. He was holding a sack.

"I noticed you did not eat the lunch. Very wise. I have brought a lunch we may share, a *croque monsieur*."

I thanked him and told him I didn't know what a *croque monsieur* is.

"It means 'crisp mister', crisp because it is fried and mister perhaps because it was the lunch of the working men. I suppose you Americans would call it a grilled ham and cheese sandwich."

I took a bite of the half sandwich he had given me. It was delicious and surprising.

"This has green *chile* in it!"

"*Oui.* It is good, no?" His accent was heavy but he seemed to relish speaking English. His vocabulary was excellent except for colloquial phrases which he tended to mangle.

"It's great. But I suspect *Cordon Bleu* would not approve of the green *chile*."

"*Au contraire.* French cooking has always been based on local ingredients. During the days of the Empire, we incorporated the ingredients of Tahiti, Quebec, Africa, Viet Nam and the Caribbean. I believe the New Mexico *chile* marries well with Gruyère."

It did indeed. We ate our sandwiches and talked of food. "Will this be on the menu?" I asked Billot.

He laughed. "No, everything is to be genuine Austrian cuisine. Tell me, Mr. Schuze, do you think the people of your state will like the Austrian dishes?"

"Please call me Hubie. An Austrian restaurant anywhere else in New Mexico would fail, but Santa Fe is not like the rest of the state. The Opera here is sold out every year. In Roswell or Farmington, getting people to listen to Mozart would require a firearm."

"I sympathize with them. I much prefer Bizet. Will the people try the food here?"

"Yes. Santa Feans have an openness to the new. Maybe they'll try it and like it."

He shook his head. "I do not think they will like it."

"Why?"

"I have eaten in the restaurants and cafés here. Even the ones that do not serve traditional New Mexican food have the local *terroir*. The corn, tomatoes, squashes and *chiles* have the freshness of the desert. This works to balance the starch. Even the meat is light because of the slow cooking methods. Austrian food is dark and heavy, like Mozart's *Requiem*."

"If you don't like Austrian food—"

"Why do I work here? Because I am traveling your country to learn about the food, and Santa Fe is on the list of cities with the best restaurants. This was the only job available. I will stay for a while. Then I go to Seattle."

"And after you have been to all the cities on your list?"

A big smile lit is face. "I will return to France and start an American restaurant."

After he left, I speculated that the sandwich was the real reason for his visit. He struck me as the sort of person who would do such small acts of kindness. I thought Molinero's talk of inspiration was nonsense, but I began to realize that I was in fact drawing inspiration from the staff. Alain Billot's appreciation of New Mexican ingredients and even Arliss Mansfield's gentle incompetence were shaping my thinking about the final product. I've always said I'm an artisan, not an artist. I know how to work with clay, and I do dead-ringer copies. But for the first time, I began to hope I did have a creative side. I wanted my design to be special.

16

When Molinero introduced Raoul Deschutes as the *poissonnier*, I assumed the term didn't mean what it sounded like. Deschutes announced the meal would be *Gebackener Karpfen*. I was avoiding M'Lanta Scruggs and had taken a seat next to Jürgen Dorfmeister who was Austrian.

"Fried carp," whispered Dorfmeister. I would rather have poison, I thought to myself. I exited the dining room and went out to the loading dock to get some fresh air.

Dorfmeister showed up a minute later. "What's wrong? You don't like fried carp?"

He had a massive head with shaggy black hair, leathery skin, a red bulbous nose and a big soft belly. He looked like the Santa from the wrong side of the tracks.

"I've never eaten carp, and I never will."

"I had it growing up," he said. "Otherwise, my childhood was happy," he added and laughed.

He lit a cigarette, and I moved a couple of feet away from him. "Will it bother you if I smoke?"

"Not so long as the smoke doesn't come my way."

He held the cigarette aloft and observed its smoke stream. "The winds seem to favor you tonight." He laughed at his joke then said, "I know it's unhealthy, but I breathe smoke all day. I figure I'd rather get lung cancer from something I enjoy than from the grilling fumes."

"So you are the grill cook."

"Yes. That pompous ass Kuchen insists on calling me the *grillardin*. But grill cook is correct." He looked at his cigarette lovingly and took a long draw. Then he looked up at me. "I am a man of large appetites, Schuze. I love red wine and scotch—not together of course." He chuckled. "I love meat, so I love my job. The only time I don't like my job is when I have to grill fish. I hate fish. But this is no problem in an Austrian restaurant. The carp is fried and the trout is smoked, so scaly creatures rarely come to my station." He crushed out the cigarette between his fingers and dropped it into a pocket in his chef pants. "Tell me about yourself. You are from New Mexico?"

"Yes, Albuquerque, about an hour south of here."

"You drive back and forth every day?"

"No, Molinero is paying for me to stay in a hotel."

"Does it have a bar?"

"Yes."

He threw his arm around my shoulders. "Then let us go."

I didn't see any way to say no, and he was an interesting guy whose company would be preferable to an empty hotel room. And since the bar was non-smoking, being with him would not be a health hazard.

Or so I thought.

When we got in the Bronco, he flipped a cigarette out of the pack, rolled down the window, and reached for the lighter only to find it was missing. Then he started looking in his pockets, I assumed for his own lighter.

"You can't smoke in my car."

"What if I sit in the back with the window down?"

I hit the button that lowers the rear window behind the back seats.

He turned when he heard the noise and saw the window's location. "You expect me to sit behind the seats?"

"If you're going to smoke."

"The bar in your hotel allows smoking?"

"No."

"I feared as much."

He exited the vehicle, walked around to the back, lowered the tailgate and climbed in. "For this humiliation, you must buy the first round."

He lit a cigarette. I drove us to the *La Fonda*. As we made our way from the parking garage to the hotel, he squeezed in one last cigarette.

I ordered a glass of Gruet. Jürgen ordered Glenmorangie single malt scotch neat—no ice, no soda, no water. According to the label, the stuff was handcrafted by the Sixteen Men of Tain. Judging by how much the bar charged for it, all sixteen of them must be millionaires.

"Why did you call Kuchen a pompous ass? Didn't you come here with him from Austria?"

He downed half of his scotch in a single gulp. "No. My father died when I was four. I scarcely remember him. When I was ten,

63

my mother married a minor functionary at the American Embassy. A year later we moved to Washington."

"The man your mother married was named Dorfmeister?"

He laughed loudly. "No, his name was Duncan. He never adopted me, so I remained Dorfmeister, which I prefer."

After the initial large slug of scotch, Jürgen switched to sipping. I asked him if it bothered him that Duncan hadn't adopted him.

"I knew nothing of these things. He was my mother's husband. He paid the rent and provided the food, and she seemed to like him. Looking back, she had no skills, so landing an American was good for her. We lived a boring middle-class life. My mother's only interests were domestic, and my father seemed to have no interests at all. I suppose his work may have occupied him well, but he never spoke of it. I wanted to *do* something, so I started cooking at home. It was the only thing my mother and I ever had in common. I left on my sixteenth birthday, and my cooking has been a passport to see the world." He turned to the bartender. "Barman, another scotch please and some snack worthy of my friend's champagne."

The bartender brought another glass of amber liquid for Jürgen and two bowls of pistachios. These strange green nuts have become all the rage since several enterprising individuals began growing them in the Tularosa Basin in the southern part of the state. I popped one in my mouth and discovered it had green *chile* flavoring. I wondered if there was anything New Mexicans wouldn't put green *chile* on.

We enjoyed an evening of multiple rounds and wide-ranging conversation. When the tab came, we each gave the bartender a credit card without looking at the total and told him to add an appropriate tip. Jürgen was too drunk to read it, and I didn't want to know. We signed our respective tabs, and Jürgen said, "I'm afraid you'll have to take me home."

"I've had too much champagne to be your designated driver."

"Then give me the keys to your vehicle."

"Jürgen, there is no way I will allow you to drive my vehicle in your condition."

He gave me a hurt look. "I'm not going to drive it. I'm going to sleep in it."

"The back window is open. Be my guest."

17

Parking garages unnerve me. Their sterile concrete environment almost invites ambush. There being no place to hide seems to apply only to the victim.

The early morning sun shown between the ramps, casting long shadows of the pillars and creating regions of pitch dark.

I approached the Bronco warily. The back window was down as I had left it, and I was happy to see Jürgen's motionless form between the tailgate and the back seat. I reached in to poke him awake, then hesitated.

During the night, he had lost about eighty pounds, and his hair had turned from black to brown.

When reason took over, I realized the body in the Bronco was not Jürgen. Then I realized it was indeed a *body*.

I don't know how I knew that, but I couldn't have been more certain of it had he sported a toe tag and been under a white sheet in the morgue. It wasn't the bump on his head—it didn't look bad enough to be fatal.

Maybe I sensed there was no rise and fall of his chest as he breathed. Maybe it was his unnaturally awkward position. Maybe it was his pallor. The skin on the back of his neck had a bluish grey tinge. In the cold night air of Santa Fe's 7200 feet, he had dropped considerably below 98.6 degrees. He was not so cold that you could use him to ice down a bottle of Gruet, but neither was he room temperature.

I stood there debating whether to touch him. If by some miracle he were alive, I didn't want him to die because I failed to seek help. So despite the fact that I was positive he was dead, and despite the fact that I hated the idea of touching a dead person, I placed my hand on his shoulder and shoved him.

"Barry?"

He didn't answer. I touched his neck. It was even colder than it looked. I went back to my room and called 911. Then I sat there wondering how a live Jürgen Dorfmeister became a dead Barry Stiles in the back of my Bronco in the parking garage of the *La Fonda*.

I figured there were three possible explanations for Stiles' death.

The least likely scenario was natural causes. He was walking through the parking garage, had a heart attack and climbed into my Bronco before he died? Someone found him dead and put him in the vehicle because he didn't want to leave the poor unlucky deceased on the floor?

The second possibility was that Barry was murdered, and someone wanted to frame me by leaving the body in my truck. Weird things like that have happened to me in the past, but I couldn't think of anyone with a motive to harm me.

The most likely explanation, I decided, was that Barry was killed for some reason having nothing to do with me. The murder took place in or near the parking garage, and the murderer selected my vehicle as a good place to dump the body because the back window was open. Even that explanation had too many coincidences. I knew the victim. He was in the parking garage of my hotel. He ended up in my Bronco.

I decided to say as little as possible to the Police.

The detective from the Santa Fe Police Department was named Danny Duran. He had a chiseled face and a bodybuilder's physique. He was about my height. His dark suit looked like it would fit me perfectly. It fit him like a wetsuit. Maybe he'd bought it before he started lifting weights. He told me the body was being taken to the morgue and my Bronco was being impounded as evidence. He was chewing gum.

"I'll need the key to your vehicle."

I had a moment of panic because I remembered Jürgen asking for my keys. Then I remembered I didn't give them to him. I found them in my jacket pocket, took the Ford key off the ring and gave it to him.

"Tell me about the body in your vehicle."

"I went to the parking garage about eight thirty. I saw the body in the back. I touched him and realized he was dead. Then I came up here and dialed 911."

He made notes as I spoke. "Where did you touch him?"

"In the parking garage." I thought that was obvious, but didn't say so.

He looked up from his note book. "Where on his *body* did you touch him?"

"Oh. On his shoulder. He was wearing a jacket. I didn't want to touch his skin."

He looked up again.

"I didn't want to touch a dead person. But then I did touch his neck just to make sure he was dead."

He nodded. "Did you know the deceased?"

"Yes. His name is . . . *was* Barry Stiles."

"How did you know him and for how long?"

"I first saw him on Friday, but I didn't meet him until Saturday. He and I were both working at *Schnitzel*, a new restaurant that hasn't opened yet."

"You a cook? A waiter?"

"No, I'm a ceramicist. I'm making plates for the restaurant."

"No kidding? I didn't know restaurants had their plates special made. How about Stiles? He helping you make plates?"

"No, he was a cook."

"So you met him three days ago?"

I nodded.

"What were the circumstances?"

"The manager of the restaurant asked the workers to give me ideas about what design to put on the plates. The cooks and other people have been dropping by as they got the chance."

"How long you two talk?"

"A couple of minutes."

"Why so short?"

"I was in a hurry to leave. I wanted to get back home. I live in Albuquerque, but I've been working up here. That's why I'm here in the hotel."

"What did he say to you?"

"He suggested a design for the plates."

I was hoping he wouldn't ask me what design Barry had suggested. I didn't want to go into the public reprimand Kuchen had delivered. But Duran was thorough.

"What design did he suggest?"

"A swastika."

He looked up from his notes. "Was he joking?"

"I don't think so."

"What was he, a skinhead or something?"

"I don't know."

"What did you say about his suggestion?"

"I ignored it. I didn't think he really wanted a swastika on the plates."

His stare suggested I was being less than totally forthcoming. Or maybe I just read that into his stare because I was.

"Then why did he suggest it?"

I didn't want to implicate anyone. I did want to tell the truth. "The head chef had criticized him rather severely in front of the whole staff. Barry was just venting his anger."

"They have a bad relationship?"

"I have no idea."

"Maybe they had a confrontation."

It wasn't a question, but he looked at me as if he expected me to confirm or deny the confrontation.

"The only time I ever saw them interact was when the chef scolded him."

Duran stared at me a few seconds more. "You see him since Saturday?"

"Yeah, I saw him at work yesterday, but we didn't speak."

"So the only time you ever spoke to him was Saturday for a couple of minutes?"

"Right."

"So how do you suppose he ended up dead in your vehicle?"

I shook my head. "I started thinking about that after I made the 911 call and calmed down."

"And?"

"I have no idea."

He stared at me. He was good at starring because he didn't blink. He chewed his gum. *Chomp, chomp.*

Finally he said, "Any theory?"

"Maybe someone put him in my Bronco because the window was down."

He stared at me some more. Then he looked down at his note pad but didn't write anything. He was reading his notes. "Don't tell anyone that Stiles was found in your vehicle."

I wanted to ask why, but all I said was, "Okay."

"And don't leave town."

"I live in Albuquerque."

"Okay, don't leave the state."

18

I walked to *Schnitzel* and discovered the police had been there and everyone knew about Barry Stiles. Presumably they didn't know where his body was found, so when the *saucier*, Maria Salazar, told me he was dead, I said that was terrible and went looking for Jürgen Dorfmeister.

I found him at his station cleaning the grills. "I need to talk to you. Outside."

"Excellent," he said. "I need a smoke."

We went to the loading dock, and I asked him if he'd actually slept in my Bronco.

He exhaled a cloud of smoke. "Only for an hour. I was freezing when I woke up. But that was good because I was sober. So I walked home."

"When was that?"

"About one o'clock."

"Did you see anyone around the truck as you left?"

"No. It was the middle of the night."

"No one outside the garage maybe?"

"Why all the questions?"

I lied. "Something is missing from the Bronco." Yeah, an explanation for why a dead man was in it, I thought to myself.

At that point, Scruggs stuck his head out and told us everyone was gathering in the dining room.

Molinero announced that the police had informed him that Barry Stiles had passed away. No one gasped. Molinero told us the cause of death had not yet been determined. An investigation was ongoing. He asked for a moment of silence. When the moment had passed, he said we would close for the day in honor of Barry and be back at work the next morning.

As people began to rise from their chairs, I blurted out "Excuse me" more loudly than I had intended. When everyone turned to me, I said, "I'd like to say something."

They sat back down. Molinero looked perplexed.

I cleared my throat. "The *Titanic* had thirty-two cooks. When it sank, thirty-one of them died. They were not fellow employees of Auguste Escoffier, but he published their pictures and biographies in his magazine. He also raised money for their families. I think we need something more than a moment of silence for Barry Stiles."

They were staring at me as if I were an idiot. I didn't blame them—I felt like one.

"What do you propose?" asked Molinero.

"I don't have a specific proposal." I looked around at the staff. "You knew him better than I did. Did he have a family? A favorite charity?"

Dead silence.

Alain Billot said to Molinero, "If you like, I could look into the matter and make a recommendation."

Molinero looked relieved. "Thank you, Alain." He looked around the room. "Does everyone find that satisfactory?"

A few heads nodded. A few faint yeses were murmured. "Fine," said Molinero, "see you all in the morning."

As people dispersed, I went to my workplace. I put the test piece with my experimental glaze into the kiln and watched as the elements began to glow.

"That was very nice of you."

I turned to see Maria Salazar in the doorway.

"It felt awkward," I said.

"But you spoke up. That's the important thing. I don't think people liked Barry very much, but he was a colleague, and we should do something." She hesitated. "I don't know what."

"Me neither. Maybe Alain will come up something."

"Maybe." She took a couple of steps into the private dining room. "I saved you a seat next to me when I saw you had been trapped by M'Lanta at the first few meals. But then you sat next to Jürgen. Maybe you two are pals?"

I laughed. "I guess we are now. Last night . . ."

I remembered I was not to tell anyone Barry was found in my Bronco, and telling her about last night would lead in that direction so I changed course and said, "Actually, I sat by him because he's Austrian, and I figured he could explain what we were eating."

"I could do that, too. I have to know all the dishes. I'm the *saucier*." She said it like she meant it. "What will you do with your day off?"

"Well, I can't go home because my truck . . ."

Oops. Can't go there either, I thought. She must be thinking I have early onset Alzheimer's and can't finish sentences.

She smiled. "Won't start? I noticed you walked to work this morning."

"I like walking, although it's cold today."

"But the sun is out. Would you like to go for a walk with me?"

"Sure. Let me get my jacket."

We walked to the Plaza, our hands in the pockets of our jackets. She asked me how I knew about Escoffier and the cooks on the *Titanic*, and I told her I'd been reading his memoires. She asked me about my work. She didn't know anything about Indian pottery, so I pointed out some of the pots in the store windows and told her about them.

She pointed to a shiny purple jug with an iridescent glaze. "What about that one?"

"That's called a *raku* glaze. That's all I can tell you about it. I only know Indian pottery."

"But it was made by an Indian. It lists his name and pueblo on the little sign there."

I squinted to read it. "So it does. But it's not traditional."

"Is that bad?"

I shrugged. "People are free to make whatever they like. I stick to traditional designs."

"You sound like Gunter," she said teasingly. "I wanted to do creative new sauces for some of the dishes, but he said, 'We must use the traditional sauces'," she said, trying to imitate his voice. "Did I sound like him?"

"No," I said, "but you did sound like Arnold Schwarzenegger."

She laughed and placed her hand inside the crook of my elbow. I escorted her around the rest of the Plaza like a gentleman. When we finished our lap, she said, "Would you like to have lunch?"

We ate at *La Casa Sena*, no doubt one of the reasons Santa Fe was on Alain Billot's list of best restaurant towns in the United States. Maria had the *poblano chile relleno* stuffed with saffron quinoa, yellow squash, crimini mushrooms, asadero cheese and something they called red *chile* tropical sauce. Her professional opinion as a *saucier* was that the sauce was perfect. She gave me a taste and I agreed. She offered me a taste of the stuffing, but I declined because it had quinoa, the eating of which I suspect explains why the Incas never developed the wheel. Quinoa has become popular in New Mexico recently, perhaps because it's related to the tumbleweed. The main difference is the tumbleweed tastes better.

I had the New Mexican trout which came with grilled asparagus, cucumber and lemon salsa, achiote and sweet pea rice and Cuban mojo. I rarely eat in restaurants. I enjoy my own cooking and don't like crowds.

La Casa Sena is crowded for good reason. The food is great. The crowd didn't bother me because we had a corner table, and I was too intent on the food and Maria to pay much attention to anything else.

I ordered a split of Gruet.

Maria countermanded my order by telling the waitress, "We'll have the full bottle." Then she looked at me and said, "Half bottles are for work days."

We talked about food. She asked if her *poblano chile* was the same thing as a *chile* she had seen in a grocery store labeled as a *pasilla*. It was, but only because the one in the store was mislabeled. I was happy to show off by explaining that a true *pasilla* ("little raisin" in Spanish) is a dried *chilaca* which is used only to make sauces. It is long and narrow whereas the *poblano* is short and wide. Confusingly, many grocery stores and even some restaurants use the words *poblano* and *pasilla* interchangeably.

We also talked about pottery, and of course we gossiped about *Schnitzel's* workforce.

I tried to get the check, but Maria insisted we split the bill. "It's lunch with a colleague," she said. "If it were a lunch date, I'd let you pay."

She smiled and my knees went weak. Maybe it was the champagne.

19

Santa Fe was at its best. Dry snow flakes floated through *piñon* scented air. The shops were gaily lit and full of holiday shoppers, some of them residents, most of them tourists taking a break from the skiing.

No one on the street knew that Barry Stiles had died. Even the people at *Schnitzel* who knew it didn't care. They had a restaurant to open.

So why did it bother me? Did Barry Stiles care that his passing left no void? Do the dead have cares?

I decided the last question was beyond my metaphysical powers, so I turned to one I might have a chance of answering. Why do we hope people will miss us and speak kindly of us when we're gone? Why do we secretly want to play Tom Sawyer and listen to our own eulogy?

The answer, I concluded, is that our concern about how we are remembered is not really about that. It's just a surrogate for caring about how we are regarded in the here and now. We don't want to be spoken of badly when we are dead because that means that now—while we are still alive—people don't like us.

I reached this profound conclusion just as I reached *La Fonda*. It was four o'clock. But it was five o'clock in Texas. That was only about 180 miles east.

Close enough. I went to the bar and ordered a bourbon on the rocks. I was in a brown mood.

An Anasazi pot sat on a flagstone mantel above the fireplace. I thought about the woman who made it. If she walked into the bar, she would recognize only two things, humans and her pot. Metal stools, glasses, lights, doorknobs and books would be no more than strange shapes to her. The same sort of thing would likely happen to us were we to return in a thousand years.

I think she would be happy to see the pot. She would ask why we have it. I would tell her we treasure it because it is a thing of beauty and because it makes us feel connected to her. I would invite her to my shop. I would ask her to make a pot in my workshop.

By the second bourbon, I had imagined the whole thing as a sequel to *Back to the Future*.

I was expelled from graduate school for digging up and selling three Anasazi pots. It wasn't illegal back then. The University thought it was immoral. I think it's immoral to leave treasure in the ground. Like Tom Sawyer, the ancient potters would love to know what we think about them. We honor them when we display their work. We dishonor them when we make modernist adaptations of it.

I was thinking of ordering a third bourbon when Jürgen Dorfmeister walked in.

"I thought you might be here," he said as he sat down next to me. He looked at my glass. "You are drinking scotch?"

"Bourbon."

"Barman," he shouted, "another bourbon for my friend and a Glenmorangie for me. Make it a double. I have some catching up to do." When the drinks came, he lifted his and said, "To the memory of Mr. Barry Stiles, *garde manger extraordinaire*."

I drank to that. I felt a little better. "Did you know him well?"

"No."

"Do you really think he was an extraordinary *garde manger*?"

"He was a man. He had feelings. He deserves a proper toast. The facts are irrelevant at such a time."

We stayed in the bar enjoying a dinner of bar foods—pistachios, salsa and chips, peanuts and some strange hard sausages. In Spain, I suppose they would have called the snacks *tapas* and charged accordingly. In the *La Fonda* they were free to their good customers, a status Jürgen and I had earned by purchasing multiple rounds of expensive beverages.

I enjoyed my time with Jürgen. He didn't ask me to drive him home. He didn't ask to sleep in my vehicle.

I left at nine-thirty to check my kiln because that was when I expected the test firing to be complete. It was cold out but I had plenty of antifreeze inside me and a good jacket outside me. I enjoyed the late-night stroll to *Schnitzel* which took only twenty minutes. I unlocked the front door and entered. Light came from the kitchen.

Even though I had a key and every right to be there, I suddenly felt like an intruder. I walked quietly to the twin swinging doors and peered through the little window in the right one, the door we were all supposed to use as an entrance only.

I didn't enter. I tiptoed to my work area and hid behind the table. The low reflected light went out. I heard footsteps. I saw a figure move silently towards the front door, open it and leave. I knew it was M'Lanta Scruggs because the light had been on in Molinero's office. It was the sight of Scruggs leaving that office that kept me from entering the kitchen and sent me scurrying behind my table.

I gave him plenty of time to vacate the neighborhood. Then I checked the kiln, decided the firing was complete and turned it off.

I went to Molinero's office and tried the door. It was locked. I tried my front door key in the lock. It didn't fit.

I went back to the hotel to think. My first thought was that Scruggs was up to no good. My second though was not actually a thought. It was a feeling—guilt at suspecting a black man of ill-doing.

So I asked myself if I would have formed the same conclusion had the person leaving Molinero's office been Arliss Mansfield. I answered myself that I would. People in someone else's office at ten o'clock at night in a dark and locked building arouse suspicion no matter what the color of their skin.

But on second thought, Scruggs might have a better reason for being there than Arliss. Maybe M'Lanta had janitorial duties in addition to his scullery work and had just finished cleaning the office. A chef is less likely to have cleaning duties than a potscrubber, so it would have been more suspicious to see Arliss in the office.

My machinations on racial profiling weren't helping me answer the one practical question confronting me—what, if anything, should I do?

20

The completion of the test firing provided an excuse to visit Molinero's office.

I found him there Wednesday morning and knocked on his door. It had a window through which I saw him as he stood up. I pretended to take his standing as permission to enter and turned the knob hard enough that it clicked.

It was locked. Molinero walked to the door, placed a key in the slot, and unlocked the door.

"Sorry, I didn't realize your door was locked. Maybe I should come back later."

"No problem," he said. "I keep the office locked at all times because the personnel files are in here."

"And the safe," I noted. It was a big one, built into the wall.

He laughed. "Yes, for keeping the hordes of cash we'll rake in starting on Monday. I see you have the charger."

"Actually, it's only a test piece." I handed it to him. "This is the background glaze I propose." I handed him a piece of paper. "This is a sketch of an edelweiss that would be in *bas* relief."

He looked at the clay and the paper. "Excellent."

"You don't want to study it for a while or talk it over with anyone?"

"No. I like the drawing. I like the glaze."

I was surprised at how easily he gave his consent for the design. I took a deep breath. I hate delivering bad news. "I can probably have four real chargers ready by Monday, so you'll have a set for one table. But it will be at least a week and maybe even two before we'll have the full one hundred."

"Even with the commercial place doing them?"

"They aren't the problem. They can glaze and fire a hundred plates in two or three days. The bottleneck is me. It will take me a long time to form the plates."

"Can't that place—clay feet?—form them?"

"Yes, but that would add to the cost. And I kind of wanted to do them myself to make sure they're right."

"I'm sure they can follow your prototype. And don't worry about the cost. We need everything to be here as soon as possible."

I was grateful he wasn't upset about the delay or the additional money. I felt guilty about the negative opinion I had formed of him.

"Anything else?" he asked.

"No. I'll start work right now on the prototype. I'll be sure to finish in time for the place to be cleaned up before we open."

"Fine."

I looked around the office for affect and asked the question I had been waiting to ask. "How do you keep your workplace so clean and neat?"

"By cleaning it myself and never letting anyone else touch anything. I'm a neat freak."

21

Breakfast was *Erdäpfellaibchen*. I skipped it because I needed to work on the plate and because I didn't like the way it sounded when it was announced.

I must have felt some sort of inspiration because I finished the plate in just over an hour. As I set it aside to dry, I thought about all the people on Molinero's list I had not consulted about the design. It was too late to make anything other than minor adjustments, but I thought I should at least get all the input Molinero had wanted me to have.

I also had another motive for wanting to talk to the rest of the staff. I thought I might learn something about Barry Stiles' death.

I knew who Helen Mure was because Kuchen had called her by name when reprimanding her and Mansfield. I found her instructing a young man how to chop bacon.

"Run a very sharp knife between the fat and lean strips." She demonstrated for him. "Then stack the lean strips and cut across them so that the resulting pieces are as close to square as you can get them. Do three pounds. Save the fats strips as well as the lean pieces."

She watched him do the first few strips then turned to me. "What can I do for you?"

She had a square face, short black hair and a nasal Midwestern accent. There was a sense of energy and tension about her.

"I came for inspiration," I said, hoping to relax her slightly.

"I don't have time for small talk."

Well, that certainly worked well. "Maybe I've come at a bad time?"

"There are no good times for a *chef de partie*."

"Then I'll let you—"

"I've got a few minutes while Pedro here chops my bacon."

"It's Juan, Ms. Mure."

"Whatever," she replied without looking at him. Then to me she said, "I have no interest in chargers or decoration generally. I cook. If you want to know something about the food that might help your work, I can answer food questions. Other than that, you are wasting your time."

"Okay, if I can know only one thing about the food you cook, what should it be?"

"It needs to be *gahm*."

I thought she said, "It needs to be gone," so I said, "In other words, you want the diners to clean their plates."

"No. The food has to be *gahm*. It's a Chinese word I learned while cooking in San Francisco. It means the flavor is not *on* the food or even *in* the food, but has become one with the food."

"Sounds very Zen," I said, not really knowing what that meant.

"Maybe, but you don't accomplish it by meditation. It's strictly a matter of technique. Two chefs start with the same piece of meat and the same seasonings. One ends up with a tasty meal you enjoy. The other ends up with a culinary experience you remember for years. The secret—like the devil—is in the details, how the meat is handled, how the seasoning is applied, the temperature at which the meat hits the pan. All these and many more factors make a huge difference."

She looked back at Juan and evidently approved of his chopping because she said nothing.

"Are you and Arliss the only two *chefs de partie?*"

Her eyes narrowed. "Why do you ask?"

Evidently, I had hit a sore spot. "No reason," I said, "Just trying to get a feel for how a place like this works."

"Okay, I'll tell you. Places like this seldom work. That fool Molinero talks about teamwork, but he knows nothing about kitchens. Kitchens are battlefields. Chefs are famous for big egos. We work in intense heat with short deadlines for everything we do. We yell and scream and insult each other."

"Wow."

"Chefs in serious restaurants adhere to certain rules—make sure health and safety procedures are rigidly maintained, treat the customer with respect and make every plate the best it can be. But between us, there are no holds barred. I was hired with the understanding that I would be one of two *chefs de partie*. Then I met that fool Mansfield and realized I was on my own. Worse, my reputation could be harmed. People don't know who cooked what. If *Schnitzel* gets a bad reputation, it will affect all of us who work here."

"Arliss seems like a nice guy," I said.

"He's a wimp. He lets Kuchen push him around. He's also slow, and that clogs us all up. But you want to know the real zinger? I think Kuchen is considering promoting Maria Salazar to *chef de partie*. She's currently the *saucier*. An appropriate title for the little tart. I'll admit she knows her job, but this promotion will be earned in the bedroom, not the kitchen."

For someone who didn't have time to talk to me, Helen had a great deal to say.

When lunch was served, Kuchen invited Mure to comment on the dish, but she said she preferred to wait until after the meal.

When the top was lifted from the elaborate tureen, I knew immediately where the chopped bacon had gone—into the *Speck-knödel*.

"It's a bacon dumpling," whispered Scruggs who had again insinuated himself next to me.

He was right, but the term 'bacon dumpling' cannot do justice to the dish Mure had prepared. Because of my interest in food, I looked up almost every item served even though most of them did not get copied into my personal cookbook. This one did, but I wondered whether I could ever duplicate what Mure had done.

It seems so simple. Stale bread, onion, bacon, warm milk, eggs, parsley, salt, pepper, nutmeg, chives and chicken broth.

Start with canned chicken broth or chicken bouillon cubes, and you might as well not bother. You already know the bacon has to be cut precisely, but you also have to figure the ration of lean to fat. The fat strips are not chopped because as you sauté the bacon you want to be able to spot them easily and pull them out when you have exactly the right amount of fat. If the temperature is allowed to climb too high, the bacon will darken too much, imparting too strong a flavor and too much crunch. Let the temperature go to low, and you'll have a fatty taste and rubbery texture.

And sautéing the bacon is just the beginning. Even small things like the parsley must be attended to with care. Chop it too soon and the oils escape. Chop it immediately before dropping it in the broth and it can add bitterness.

When I sipped the first spoonful of broth around the dumplings, I knew what Helen meant by *gahm*. It was not merely a liquid with great flavor. It was a spoonful of pure flavor. The chicken, bacon, onions and other flavors had coalesced into a new and wonderful thing.

When Helen stood up, there was spontaneous applause. She bowed and sat down without saying a word.

I thought about the breakfast casserole Miss Gladys had brought me on Sunday. It, too, started with stale bread. I pictured Ms. Helen Mure and Miss Gladys Claiborne going head-to-head at the Pillsbury Bake-off and chuckled. Then I wondered if Helen Mure had gone head-to-head with Barry Stiles. They were both hot-tempered. Not much to go on, but enough to put her on the suspect list.

22

I called Rafael Pacheco after lunch and told him about Barry's death. I urged him to come up and meet Molinero and Kuchen because they needed to make an emergency hire before the Grand Opening on Monday. He promised to be there at nine the next morning.

For dinner that night, Kuchen announced *Buergenlandische Gaenseleber* prepared by Alain Billot with a special sauce by Maria Salazar. I turned to Scruggs. "Goose liver and onions," he said. I left the table.

Two hours later Maria entered my work area. "Slaving over a hot kiln?"

She didn't look like someone who would seduce Kuchen to get promoted. She was pretty enough to seduce anyone, but she looked too fresh and wholesome to do so. Like one of the Von Trapp daughters all grown up, but that was probably just because I had been working on edelweiss designs. Or is the plural edelweissen? Edelweißes?

"I'll get you a chair," I offered.

"Don't bother," she said and plopped down on the floor. She crossed her ankles in front of her, holding them in her hands, knees sticking out to the side like a little girl. She blew a few strands of hair off her face. She smiled at me. "Why did you skip dinner?"

"I don't like liver."

"It was goose liver. Have you ever tasted it?"

"No."

"Well, don't think of the awful liver and onions your mother made you eat."

"My mother never made me eat anything."

"You must have been a spoiled child," she said breezily.

"Terribly," I said.

"I'm going to bring you some food," she said and popped up like a Jill-in-the-box before I could protest.

She returned ten minutes later with a sandwich of sliced goose liver dressed with a dark sauce between two slices of crusty bread. I feared the liver would deliver the *coup de grâce* to my *système digestif*, but food was exactly what my tummy needed in order to attack something other than itself.

The creamy liver and crunchy bread were a delicious combination. The dark sauce would have made a bicycle tire tasty. Maria was right—this was nothing like the dreaded calf's liver.

"What's in this sauce?"

"A *saucier* never tells," she said with a look on her face that indicated maybe she did.

"Speaking of *sauciers*, I hear you may be in line for a promotion to *chef de partie*."

A frown passed over her face, and I noted she was just as attractive frowning as she was smiling.

"That wouldn't be a promotion in my mind. I love sauces, and

I don't want to stand over a stove and under a salamander for hours on end. Where did you hear this?"

"A potter never tells."

"*Touché*. Okay, I'll tell you what's in the sauce and you tell me who said I might become a *chef de partie*." It had the flirty tone one might associate with "I'll show you mine if you'll show me yours."

I didn't want to tell her for fear of causing friction among the staff. There was too much of that already. But she started explaining the sauce, and I couldn't bring myself to interrupt because she was so exuberant. Also, I wanted to know what was in it.

She recited the ingredients—shallots, honey, verjus and veal stock. Oops. Can't serve that to Susannah. Maybe a good chicken stock would work. Then she said, "Okay, your turn. Who told you I might become a *chef de partie*?"

What to do? I hadn't twisted Helen Mure's arm to make her talk, and she hadn't sworn me to secrecy. There was nothing to prevent me from telling Maria the truth.

I told her half of it—that Mure had mentioned it as a possibility. I didn't tell her Mure's opinion of how Maria was likely to "earn" the promotion.

She was surprised by the news but didn't seem angry. "I wonder why she would say that?"

The question wasn't directed to me so I didn't answer it.

"Let's make a game of this," she suggested. "I'll tell you why I think she said it, and then you tell me if it makes sense."

I didn't like where this was going. "I wouldn't have any way of knowing if it makes sense. I'm just an interloper."

"No, she told you for a reason. And you'll know my theory makes sense if it fits with the way she told you—the words she used, the tone of her voice."

"I don't think—"

"But first I have to swear you to secrecy," she said with mock seriousness.

"Why? You're not telling me a secret, just a theory."

"When you hear it, you'll know why. Promise not to tell?"

She was irresistible. I crossed my heart, sealed my lips and threw away the key.

"I think she wants me to be a *chef de partie* so that we have to work side by side. She likes me."

Her theory made no sense at all. Not only did Mure not like Salazar, she seemed to despise her.

"That's a surprising theory," I said.

"That's because you don't know how I know she likes me. That's the secret part." She paused for effect then announced, "She's been hitting on me ever since I arrived."

I guess I looked dumbfounded because after a few seconds of silence she said, "You're surprised, aren't you?"

"Yes. Somehow I got the impression you liked Kuchen."

She furrowed her brow. "I can't imagine any woman falling for someone that conceited and domineering."

Despite her girlish demeanor, she looked up close to be in her mid thirties. Her black hair reached just above her shoulders and then turned up and inward. I suppose getting it to stay that way involved the use of a spray or curlers or a permanent or one of those processes I know nothing about, but it looked free and loose and not stiff at all.

I was drawn to her, and that made me nervous. She didn't seem the type to commit a murder, but what if she and Barry had a stormy romance? Susannah tells me that love and money are the only motives for murder.

23

It snowed overnight, but Rafael was at the entrance of *Schnitzel* when I arrived shortly before nine.

He was huddled against the door blowing on his hands to keep them warm. "Neither rain nor cold nor dark of night," he said as I unlocked the door.

The only other person early to work was M'Lanta Scruggs. "I brewed fresh coffee," he said.

"Great," I said and started towards the kitchen.

"I'll bring it to you," he said, stepping into my path. "How you like it?"

"Cream and sugar," said Rafael.

"Black," I said.

"Like your girlfriend," he said.

Rafael and I went to my work area. "What was that about?"

"He was giving me a hard time about not knowing any blacks, so I told him I'd dated a black girl."

"I can see that broke the ice."

I liked this guy. "I'm sorry I kept you waiting out in the cold."

"I was early. And it gave me time to figure out whether a battering ram or a catapult would be the best way to get in."

"It is an imposing entry," I agreed.

"You almost expect armed guards and customs agents waiting to stamp your passport."

I showed him my charger design. He said it was great for an Austrian restaurant, but why would we have one in New Mexico?

"At least they have cold dishes other than *guacamole* and salsa," I pointed out.

"How about warm dishes?"

"There's *Liptauer*."

"What's her first name?"

"Huh?"

He laughed. "I meant warm dishes on the staff, not on the menu."

"Oh."

"Tell me about *Liptauer*."

"It's a cheese dip."

"And I thought Austrian food would take me away from all that. Is it made by Frito Lay?"

"It tastes like it might be, but don't say that to Kuchen. It has quark, capers and paprika."

"Isn't quark a subatomic particle?"

"I think it's cream cheese in this case. If Kuchen asks you about it, be sure to say that draining the capers is important to avoid a vinegar taste. Also, the paprika should be subtle, not overpowering."

"Who knew? How did you learn all this?"

"Barry served it, and I listened to Kuchen berate him."

Scruggs came in with our coffee.

Rafael asked, "Are you the barista?"

"No. I'm the potscrubber."

Rafael took a sip. "You deserve a promotion."

"Why you think anything from potscrubber is a promotion?"

After he walked away, Rafael turned to me. "Sensitive type, isn't he?"

"So I've discovered. And he's the most normal guy here."

He held his cup up in a mock salute. "Here's to *la vida loca*."

He had a sort of cheeky humor I appreciated, but I was beginning to fear he might have an unsavory side.

Raoul Deschutes came in and said, "Sorry, I didn't know you had a guest."

"Yes, someone who wants to meet you." I introduced them and explained that Rafael was interested in the *garde manger* position.

Raoul's face darkened.

Rafael said quickly, "Hubie told me about the position before Barry Stiles died. He thought the position might come open because Chef Kuchen seemed displeased with Barry. I was interested, but of course I never would have approached Kuchen while Barry was still here. Barry and I worked together at Café Alsace. Even if we hadn't, you don't undermine another worker even in our cutthroat business."

"*Oui*, it is cutthroat, and the biggest cutter of throats is Kuchen himself. I wouldn't be surprised if he killed Stiles."

I wondered briefly if he said that to throw suspicion away from himself. Of course there was no reason to suspect Deschutes. In fact, there was no good reason to suspect anyone. For all I knew, Barry choked to death on a *schnitzel*.

Rafael and I glanced at each other.

"I want the position, but it feels ghoulish to apply the day after the guy who had it died."

Deschutes demonstrated the Gallic shrug. "Life goes on. As does the business of cooking. We need to open so the pay will begin."

"But you're all getting stipends, right?" ask Rafael.

"Yes, but paid in arrears."

Rafael and Raoul chatted about their work experience. Raoul seemed happy to give a quick tutorial, although it was clear he didn't think Austrian food was *haute cuisine*. As other people trickled in, I introduced them to Pacheco. I stood around during those brief chats until we got to Kuchen.

I left them alone and returned to my space where I applied the slip glazes and put the plate in the kiln. Watching a plate fire is no more riveting than watching one dry. I went for a walk. As I left the building, I saw Rafael and a woman who looked like Vivien Leigh leaning in close to him near the empty bar, radiant smiles on both their faces.

24

I returned to my workspace to find it a considerably more pleasant sight than it had been when I left.

Not because someone had cleaned it. Scarlett O'Hara was standing in the middle of it.

"Wallace Voile," she said and extended her hand. She allowed me to hold it briefly. "I understand everyone was asked to speak with you about the chargers."

She had a low voice and perfect diction. Her skirt hugged perfect hips without being tight enough to be tacky. A white blouse was tucked in so perfectly as to appear sewn to the skirt.

"I'd like to talk with you about the chargers, but it's too late. The prototype is in that kiln."

"Bad timing on my part," she said with a practiced smile. "I've never been involved in any sort of design for the restaurants where I worked, so I was rather looking forward to it."

"I understand one of the places you worked was Café Alsace."

Her lips formed a curious smile. "How did you know that?"

"Rafael Pacheco told me."

"Yes, he was our *garde manger*," she said in a voice that gave away nothing about her opinion of Rafael.

"He's interviewing here to replace Barry Stiles," I said.

"I'm sure Barry's death has been a shock to us all," she said, making no reply to my comment about Rafael's interview. If she were shocked by Barry's death, she had not allowed that emotion to affect her mellifluous voice. Nor her eyes, which also reflected no shock. Nor sadness. Nor any other emotion.

"I know I was shocked," I said.

"It was nice to meet you, Mr. Schuze." She allowed me to hold her hand again and glided away.

I thought of her and Rafael together in the bar. He had the nickname, but she had the persona. Was it also the persona of a murderer?

25

The Santa Fe Police Department released my Bronco. Scruggs loaded the kiln and roller into it. Rafael and I managed the wheel this time in addition to the extension cord.

I packed the glazing materials in several wooden produce boxes scavenged from the dumpster by the loading dock. I cleaned the shelves and rolled them to the storage room. I folded the tarps and placed them on the shelves.

On my way back from the storage room, I took a last look into my work area to make sure I hadn't forgotten anything and was surprised to see Machlin Masoot with a bewildered look on his face.

He smiled when he saw me. "Wallace Voile said I am too late to help you with the design." He was holding a tray. "I have brought a gift of appeasement."

It was a Linzer torte, the first dish at *Schnitzel* I could pronounce. The French Café in *La Fonda* bakes them. You can even find them at the bakery in the Smith's Grocery on Yale Boulevard near Tristan's apartment. They look like an ordinary fruit pie with the typical latticework crust, so I had never bothered to try one.

Masoot's Linzer tortes were sized as individual servings, the pie version of a cup-cake. I didn't know what to call them. I don't suppose cup-pie is a word?

When I took a bite, I knew why Kuchen was so proud of his *patisserie*. I always thought of crusts as simply vessels for the filling, but Masoot's crust was the main event, a crumbly, rich, spicy, nutty mixture that made me want to learn how to bake it so I could have it with Gruet.

I thought he was going to dance when I told him how much I liked it. He swayed from side to side and seemed to be going up and down on his toes.

"It is named for my city, Linz."

"I didn't know that."

"Yes. It is the oldest tort in the world. *Wie mann die Linzer Dortten macht* dates back to 1653."

I told him that was amazing because I figured it was easier than asking him what the devil he was talking about. I wanted to eat, not talk. Alas, the torts were small and too soon gone.

"You are leaving us?"

"Just for the weekend. I'll be here for the grand opening on Monday."

"You will bring the chargers?"

"I'm afraid not. They won't be ready for a week or more."

"Was Molinero upset by the delay?"

"No."

"Hmm. What about Kuchen?"

"I don't think he knows yet."

Masoot gave me a conspiratorial smile. "Perhaps it will be better if you are not here when he hears this news."

"Yes. He is quite the stickler for schedules."

"And for loyalty. If I were you, I'd keep what I know to myself."

"That's easy," I said. "I don't know anything."

"Also, be careful what you say to Voile."

"Why?"

He looked around then lowered his voice. "I believe she is the paramour of Molinero. I saw them embrace."

I found it hard to believe that Voile would be attracted to Molinero. But then Mure had told me Maria had a thing with Kuchen, and that turned out to be false. Unless Maria had lied about it. There was entirely too much gossip at *Schnitzel*.

I asked Masoot if I could borrow three things for the weekend. The first was an industrial-size pot. The second was a set of cookie sheets. The last was a plastic container with a tight fitting lid into which I transferred the barium carbonate because the container it came in must have had a leak. The level was lower than I remembered, and I was worried there might not be enough left for a hundred chargers. The last thing I wanted was a further delay waiting for more glazing supplies.

The Gruet Winery is on Interstate 25 on the north side of Albuquerque. They have a tasting room, but I already knew what it tasted like. Which is why I stopped there and bought a case of *Blanc de Noir*. Then I dropped off the prototype charger, clay and glazing materials at Feats of Clay and headed for Old Town.

26

The tang of tomatoes and onions played against the earthy scents of *masa* steaming in the kitchen and *piñon* drifting from the *kiva* fireplace. A perfect margarita—silver tequila from blue agave, lime juice and triple sec—was in my hand, the glass crowned by a jagged line of coarse salt.

The lithesome Angie had delivered more chips, and Susannah was foraging. She has this theory that chips soak up the alcohol and keep you from getting drunk.

"Being away from this place for a week was almost more than I could stand."

"It wasn't a week. It was only four days, less than that when you consider you didn't get there on Monday until lunchtime."

"It seemed longer. But it will all be over on Monday." I raised my glass. "To my last day at *Schnitzel*."

She clinked her glass against mine. Little did we know.

"How is Ice doing?" she asked.

"Fine," I said, feeling guilty about not saying something about him and Voile. But for all I knew, they were just chatting about old times at Café Alsace, and I would have felt even worse had I inadvertently borne false witness against him.

Wanting to change the subject, I told her I was surprised the Grand Opening was on a Monday and wondered why it wasn't on a Saturday, the busiest day for restaurants.

"I suspect they chose Monday because that's the night most restaurants close. They'll have the Santa Fe foodies all to themselves."

"You think people will come?"

"Of course they will. It's 'The City Different'. A new restaurant always draws a crowd. Plus, the publicity about Barry Stiles only adds to the intrigue."

"That's a sad thought. I was dejected that Barry's death had no impact. But I guess it did—it was free advertising."

"What was he like?"

"I don't know. We had only that one brief conversation after Kuchen humiliated him. Three days later he was dead in the back of the Bronco."

"And you still think someone killed him and put him in your vehicle because the window was down?"

I nodded.

"That's lame even by your standards."

Susannah loves mysteries almost as much as she loves romances. "You have a better theory?"

"A body turned up once in Bernie Rhodenbarr's bathroom. It was someone he and Carolyn met by accident while waiting in the ticket line at a museum. I guess in New York people actually stand in line to get in a museum."

"In Santa Fe, too."

"Anyway, Bernie barely knew the guy—just like you and Barry—but do you think he wrote it off as coincidence? No way. He knew there had to be a connection."

"Bernie Rhodenbarr is a fictional character, Suze."

"I know that, but life imitates art."

"I thought it was the other way around."

"It is. Oscar Wilde said, 'Art imitates life, and life imitates art'."

"He did?"

"Carolyn discovered the body slumped on the toilet when she went to use the bathroom. Ray Kirschmann was in the store and also wanted to use the bathroom, so she stayed in there hoping he would leave. But he kept waiting so—"

"Who's Ray Kirschmann?"

"He's the cop."

"Oh, right." I read one of those books at Susannah's insistence, but I have to admit I didn't commit the *dramatis personae* to memory.

"So he keeps hanging around, and finally Carolyn comes out and tells Bernie the toilet is overflowing. Bernie asks Kirschmann if he'll help clean it up, and of course Ray beats it out of there."

"I just know there's a reason you're telling me this."

"Just try to follow it, okay? Carolyn had been stalling because she knew Bernie was going to be a suspect. The toilet malfunction was just a ruse because she didn't want Kirschmann to find the body."

I was waiting for the punch line but didn't know if I'd recognize it when it came.

"So?"

"So if there was no connection, she would have just said, 'Hey, Ray, it's a good thing you're here because I just found a dead guy in the bathroom'."

She smiled as if that made sense. Maybe it did. "How does this relate to Barry Stiles?"

"You're going to be a suspect, Hubie, because Barry has a connection to you and was found in your Bronco just like the dead artist had a connection to Bernie and was found on his toilet."

"The dead guy was an artist?"

"Sort of. He was being paid to forge Mondrians. That's what got him killed."

I signaled Angie for a refill. I had been sipping while Susannah outlined most of Lawrence Block's plot. You should be thankful I spared you the part where Carolyn's cat was abducted, and the woman who called about a ransom had a Nazi accent.

Susannah studied my expression. "What's wrong?"

"I don't like stories where people who make copies get killed."

27

I left Tristan a message saying I'd be in the shop on Friday, so he needn't come in.

He left me something better—five thousand dollars hidden away in the *caja fuerte* in my secret compartment. He's the only person in the world other than me who knows where it is and how to open it. If I get hit by lightning, he can find the papers he needs to sell off the merchandise and the building. Or he can go into the pot-selling business. Make that '*pottery*-selling' business.

If we both get zapped by the same bolt, I guess the papers will stay in the wall until some jackass anthropologist discovers them. He'll probably decide they aren't worth studying and return them to some dig site being filled in to protect it from treasure hunters.

The five thousand was from the sale of a Laguna jug. I was confident it was from the early nineteenth century. I was less confident about the pueblo. Laguna pottery from that era is so similar to the work from Acoma that it's almost impossible to be certain unless you know the pot's provenance. I didn't in this case. I had bought it at a garage sale for a hundred dollars.

The pottery business can be profitable at times.

It felt good to be back behind my counter. Tonight would be the first Friday in December, the night of the annual Holiday Stroll in Old Town, billed by the merchants association as Albuquerque's Biggest Christmas Party. There would be dancers and musicians. The Albuquerque Fire Department Color Guard would be there to raise the flag and play the National Anthem. Of course the politicians would be out, almost certainly the mayor and local members of the State Legislature. Probably some officials from the tribal councils at Isleta and Sandia. Maybe even one of our senators.

Susannah agreed to adjust our cocktail hour to coincide with the speeches by the politicians. But we would be out in time to watch the lighting of the giant Christmas tree at Plaza Don Luis and to see Santa Claus parade around the Plaza.

Then we'd both go to work. Susannah had agreed to work the late evening shift because the restaurant expected a big crowd and she expected big tips.

I wanted to stay open myself because for most Old Town merchants, this is the biggest day of the year. I never know how my shop, Spirits in Clay, will do. With the cheapest piece at a thousand dollars, no one buys stocking stuffers from me.

But I've had Holiday Stroll nights when as many as three discriminating shoppers have purchased genuine traditional Indian pottery for someone on Santa's 'nice' list. Or perhaps someone who has been delightfully naughty.

When the crowd grew less rowdy around six, I knew the speeches were about to begin, so I hustled over to *Dos Hermanas* where our table was waiting.

We got angry looks from a few of the people in line when Angie showed us to our table. Others in the line seemed to be studying us to determine if we were celebrities.

Susannah said, "The *luminarias* are so beautiful."

"I know. They always put me in the Christmas spirit."

"Who's on your list this year?"

Our margaritas arrived without us placing an order, probably reinforcing the opinion of those in line who thought we were big shots.

"The usual suspects—Tristan, Martin, Consuela and Emilio, Miss Gladys, Father Groas and a young lady from Willard."

Although it is the closest town to her family home, Susannah isn't actually from Willard. She grew up on a ranch twelve miles south/southwest of that sleepy village, but I like saying she's from Willard because we both think it's a funny name.

"Didn't you leave someone out?"

I thought about it briefly. "Angie?"

"I meant Dolly."

"Oops."

"You do remember her, right?"

"The list has been the same for the last several years. I didn't know Dolly last Christmas."

"So what will you get her? An engagement ring?" she joked.

"Maybe."

She almost dropped her drink. "Are you serious?"

"Maybe. At least I've been thinking about it. And about the future." Mainly I had been thinking about the future of Consuela Sanchez who, as Consuela Saenz, had arrived at the Schuze household shortly after the stork. Consuela was my nanny, older sister and second mother. She left to marry Emilio Sanchez when I left for college. Kidney disease was threatening her life, but she never dwelled on it.

"I've been thinking about Consuela. About how she never worries about her own health. She worries that Ninfa won't give her a grandchild. She worries that she isn't able to take care of Emilio. She has a family to care about."

"Wow. This doesn't sound like you."

"I know. Happy-go-lucky bachelor and all that. But the big five-o is approaching, and my biological clock is ticking."

"Men don't have biological clocks. Guys can father a child at almost any age. All you have to do is to meet the right woman and not be afraid to pop the question when you do."

She regarded me for a few seconds as if I were an object of study. "I know why you forgot to add Dolly to your Christmas list. You were subconsciously thinking about your date with Maria Salazar."

"It wasn't a date. It was just lunch."

She laughed a knowing laugh. "That's what *you* think."

"That's also what Maria thought," I countered. "When they brought the check, she insisted we split it because it was just two colleagues having lunch together."

"You really are clueless. It may suit her purposes to let you think it wasn't a date, but she came on to you, right?"

"It seemed like it, but maybe that was just wishful thinking."

"Or the male ego at work."

I admitted the possibility. "Anyway, it doesn't matter. I'm dating Dolly."

"You've dated two women at the same time."

"Never."

"What about Dolly and Izuanita?"

"I never dated Izuanita."

"Right. You just had lunch with her. If Ice kept having lunch with other girls, I'd consider that dating."

I said to myself, *What about standing real close to them in a very friendly discussion?* I said to Susanna, "Has he been having lunch with other girls?"

"I have no idea. It was just an example. We aren't exclusive or anything."

"Then you're not upset with me for suggesting he move from *La Placita* to *Schnitzel*?"

"Not at all. In fact, you did us both a favor. Romances between restaurant staff are notoriously stormy. Now that he's working somewhere else, we won't have that problem."

"So I guess it would be safe to date Maria after Monday when I won't be working at *Schnitzel*?" I joked.

She gave me one of her mischievous smiles, only one side of her lips turned up and her eyes squinty. "Not while you're in a 'relationship'."

I put my margarita down and leaned back in my chair. Or tried to. It's not easy in the ladder backs at *Dos Hermanas*.

"Like I said, I've been thinking about my current 'relationship'."

"That could be good. Maybe it means Dolly is the right woman."

"Evidently a string of other guys thought so."

"Not nice, Hubert."

"Sorry. You're right—the issue isn't how many times she's been married. That's her business. The issue is whether she's the right one."

She sighed. "You're asking the wrong person. The list of guys I've thought were the right one includes a married guy, a gay guy and a murderer."

"Well, at least you've been looking, so maybe you can help me with this. See, I never looked at dating that way. I don't go out with someone with the aim of finding out if she's the one. I go out with a woman because she's fun and interesting. To put it bluntly, I've never shopped for a wife."

"Oink."

"I said it was blunt."

"Oinky, too. Did you grow up wanting to be a bachelor?"

"No. I assumed I would be married like everyone else."

"And how did you think that would happen if you didn't 'shop for wife' on your dates?"

"I just figured it would happen. What did I know? I didn't date much in high school except before big algebra tests. That's when the girls would smile and speak to me."

"That's sad, Hubie."

"I didn't see it that way. I liked being more popular than the jocks even if for only a few days. And I got to smooch with a few of the girls after the tutoring sessions."

"Define 'smooch'."

"A few kisses behind the 510 shelves in the library."

"The 510 shelves?"

"The Dewey Decimal number for math books."

"Jeez. And it never even crossed your mind to wonder if one of those girls would end up as your wife?"

"I was a teenager. I figured I'd meet my wife when I was really old, like thirty."

She shook her head slowly. "No wonder relations between the sexes are so messed up. Girls grow up dreaming of being married, and guys grow up dreaming of being sports stars and assuming a beautiful wife will plop into their lives at some point."

"That was me, except for the sports star part. But it hasn't happened, so I have to do something about it or grow old alone."

"You have to shop for a wife."

"Forget I said that."

"Which brings me back to my question. Is Dolly the one?"

"That's the problem. I don't know. She's a nice person. She has a sense of humor. She's sexy."

"Well if nice, funny and sexy don't give you a clue, what else are you looking for?"

"Fabulously wealthy would be nice."

She threw a chip at me, and I amazed both of us by catching it.

I decided to hazard a serious answer to her question. "Dolly is fun to be with now because we're dating. We're together only for special events, so to speak, one of us cooking and the other being a guest. Or we go to the Balloon Fiesta or see a movie. But if we were married, we'd be together all the time."

"And that would be bad?"

"I don't know. We don't have many interests in common. She likes decorating, gardening and watching television. I like reading and watching the stars. She's not interested in Indian pottery or anthropology. If I bring up one of my anthropological theories, she listens politely, but she's obviously not interested."

"She's not the only one whose eyes glaze over when you start explaining one of your theories."

"I know. But it's not just anthropology. She doesn't seem interested in abstract ideas generally. When you see a painting, you think about what it means, what the artist was trying to do. When Dolly sees it, she wonders if it would look good over the sofa."

"That's an awful thing to say."

"I didn't mean it as an insult. I don't think less of her because she's not an art historian or an anthropologist. But when I think of marriage, I wonder what we'd talk about."

"My parents talk about the weather and the chores they have for the day."

"Mine talked about what they had done during the day. They had a cocktail hour just like we do."

"So neither of our parents talked about big abstract ideas. But my parents have a great marriage and so did yours."

She was right. "There's something else," I said. "It seems . . . I don't know, illogical I guess, that now that I'm thinking about marriage, the person I happen to be dating goes to the top of the list. Maybe the other women I've dated would be a better match, but I don't know it because I wasn't thinking about marriage when I was with them."

"So what's your plan, Hubert? You want to go out with all your exes again to make sure you didn't miss something?"

"No, of course not," I said emphatically. Then in my Groucho Marx voice, I said, "But there were a couple of them that might make me say the magic woid."

She laughed and said I sounded nothing like Groucho Marx. I pointed out that I must have because she knew who I was *trying* to sound like.

"So why don't you start dating some other women? Don't rush into anything, but just see how it feels to think of someone as a potential wife."

"I can't date other women while I'm with Dolly."

She stared at me for a few seconds. "You haven't said anything to Dolly that would make her think you don't date other women, have you?"

"No, but we've been dating for three or four months and we sleep together, so in my view it would be wrong for me to start dating other people."

"What if you told her?"

"That I was going to date other women?"

"Yes."

"That would be cruel. I couldn't do it."

"So you've never broken off a relationship?"

"You know I have. You were there when I ended it with Stella Ramsey. That was tough. But I can do that. If I decided to break up with Dolly and had a good reason for doing so, I could do it. But I couldn't look her in the eyes and tell her I want to date other women."

"Why don't I meet guys like you, Hubie?"

"You like wishy-washy guys?"

Her laughter ended in one of those crooked smiles except with her big brown eyes wide and bright. "I know a good reason for you to break up with Dolly."

I could tell she was joking, so I played along. "Yeah?"

"Yeah, that legion of husbands." She leaned over the table towards me, still smiling. "Come on, aren't you curious about how many?"

28

Over a hundred people passed through Spirits in Clay Friday night. Not one of them made a purchase.

As they exited the store, many of them said they might come back later. None of them did.

It was a little depressing, but I had the five thousand from Tristan's sale, less the commission I had decided to pay him.

I sometimes don't open on Saturdays until noon, but the Saturday after Holiday Stroll is usually busy, so I decided I'd open at ten. In order to fortify myself for the onslaught of customers, I ate some breakfast tacos. I had only one glass of Gruet because it was a work day. I crammed a whole chicken in a glass bowl just large enough to hold it. I filled the bowl with lime juice and put it in the fridge. I was hoping to wow Dolly that evening with what I call *Ave Tampico*.

Then I opened and sat there watching the shoppers pass by.

Martin showed up at noon, which was convenient for him because I was fixing lunch and for me because I needed the roller back in my workshop and the kiln back in my patio. Martin is my height but about thirty pounds heavier, all of it muscle, so he was the right man for the job.

"How'd you get this kiln in the truck?"

"The head dishwasher helped me."

"Meaning he put it in and you watched."

"I had to carry the extension cord."

"So you exploited the lowest-skilled worker in the restaurant."

"You expect one of the chefs to carry a kiln?"

"Good point."

After he brought the slab roller in, I said, "The last time you came, I gave you breakfast. Now I'm making you a lunch. You out of groceries on the Rez?"

"I didn't come for lunch. I came to bring your dog home."

"So you're not going to eat lunch?"

"Of course I am. It's payment for keeping him."

"Was he a good doggie?" I asked as I rubbed him behind the ears and deftly avoided being licked on the mouth.

"He didn't chase the livestock or pee in the house."

"He's a gentleman."

"He also didn't chase the prairie dogs or the lizards and there were a lot of them running around. He seems to be missing his chase instinct."

"What about a stick?"

"Sticks don't run," he said deadpan.

I told him about seeing M'Lanta Scruggs coming out of Molinero's office in the middle of the night.

"The dishwasher you made carry the kiln?"

"I didn't make him do it. He volunteered. I like the guy, although I suspect he'd be surprised to hear it. He has a chip on his shoulder, but he seems honest and straightforward. And unlike most others *at Schnitzel,* he doesn't gossip or complain. He certainly doesn't seem the type to break into his boss' office."

"Maybe he was just cleaning up."

"I thought of that, but at ten at night? Also, I asked Molinero later how he keeps his office so neat, and he said, 'By cleaning it myself and never letting anyone else touch anything'."

"Hmm. Maybe Molinero left the door open by mistake and Scruggs was closing it like a Good Samaritan."

"He could close it, but he couldn't lock it. When Molinero let me into his office, he had to use a key to unlock it even from the *inside.* It's a double-cylinder dead bolt."

"And when you tried the door after Scruggs left, it was locked?"

"Right."

"Maybe he picked the lock."

"Yeah, like Bernie Rhodenbarr."

"Who is Bernie Rhodenbarr?"

"A friend of Susannah's," I said.

After Martin left, I called Dolly. She asked for a rain check because her father was having a difficult day and needed her help.

29

Father Groas dropped by that evening.

"You missed Saturday Mass again, Youbird."

"Don't you normally hear confessions at this time?"

"Yass, but evidently everyone wass good this week," he said and laughed his deep rumbling laugh.

I offered him a beer.

"Perhaps would not mix well with consecrated wine," he replied.

San Felipe de Neri church in Old Town was founded in 1706 and has a strange enough history that Father Groas seems to fit right in.

In 1715, a local criminal was exiled to El Paso. He escaped on his way and took sanctuary in the church, which he evidently thought preferable to life in El Paso.

It rained so much in 1792 that the walls of the church collapsed. No doubt the climate scientists of the day were warning of global monsooning. New adobe walls were built five feet thick.

Around 1850, a Frenchman, Father Machebeuf, became the first non-Spaniard priest at Neri. Italian priests arrived twenty years later. Now we have Groas, originally from Romania. Or maybe The Ukraine. It doesn't matter because his allegiance is to the Rusyns, a people without a country, and don't get him started on their history.

The Good Father is over six feet tall, weighs in at around two forty and has a thick bushy beard. He speaks English like Béla Lugosi.

"I have some ethical dilemmas, Father."

"You want to make confession?"

"I'm not a Catholic."

He smiled broadly. "Is probably why you miss Mass."

I told him about seeing Scruggs leaving Molinero's office and asked if he thought I should say something to Molinero or even to the police.

He shook his head. "Is only one person you can tell—Mr. Scruggs."

The idea of confronting Scruggs was terrifying. "Can I just say nothing?"

"Yass. There may be an innocent reason for Mr. Scruggs being there. Bot if your conscience says you must do something, you must start by giving Mr. Scruggs a chance to explain before you accuse him to a third person."

I knew he was right. I told him next about seeing Rafael with Wallace Voile.

He stroked his beard and said nothing.

"Same answer?" I asked.

He nodded.

Great. So now I had to confront both Scruggs and Pacheco. Or call it none of my business and not stick my nose in.

"I saved the biggest one for last," I said and told him about Dolly. Having decided that I should at least think about marriage, I asked him how I would know if Dolly is the right woman. And if she isn't—or even if I'm just unsure—how do I go about finding the one who is?

"Do you want to ask her to wait while you see if someone else should be your wife?"

"No."

"I did not think so. So again the answer is obvious."

"I have to either marry her, decide to remain single, or break it off."

He nodded again.

"You are a wise man, Father."

"I tell you only what you already know. Is same for confession. People come because they know they have sinned. They do not need me to tell them this. They need me to listen. Then I tell them what they should do to atone."

"You left out that last part for me," I said.

"You have nothing so far to atone for in these cases. You should pray about it, Youbird."

A few customers drifted in after he left. When one drifted out empty handed around four, I closed the door behind him and rotated the sign to 'closed'.

I took the chicken out of the fridge, dumped out the lime juice, and left the chicken on the counter so it could come up to room temperature.

I took Geronimo for a walk. But first I waited for him to poop in the patio because I resolved long ago, when I first saw someone doing it, that I would never walk around behind an animal carrying a plastic bag and a little scoop. I mean, what must the dog think when we do that? I still have to scoop it up, but I don't have to bag it and carry it around like a souvenir.

When we got back, I rubbed the chicken with corn oil. I cooked up a simple sauce of honey, smoked paprika, fresh ginger and lime juice (newly squeezed—never cook with liquids in which a chicken has been marinating).

While the chicken roasted, I read some more of Escoffier's *Memories of My Life*. I can't say it was exciting reading, but some of it was interesting. For example, he was short like me and wore platform shoes so that he could work more easily on the burners of the stoves. He began restaurant work when he was only thirteen, starting as an assistant to the *saucier* but was taught all aspects of restaurant operations. When he was nineteen, the owner of *Le Petit Moulin Rouge*, one of the finest restaurants in Paris according to the book, was dining where Escoffier worked. Evidently a man who knew talent when he saw it, he hired Escoffier on the spot as his *sous-chef*.

When I was nineteen, I was a sophomore in college and had never worked a day in my life. The only thing I could cook was popcorn. Escoffier at that age had worked for six years and was second in command at a major Parisian restaurant. He eventually became director of kitchens at such world-famous hotels as the Grand Hotel at Monte Carlo and the Savoy and Carlton in London. I became a pot thief. Perhaps a hard early life does stiffen the character.

Every few pages, I would take a break and baste the chicken with the sauce. The evening progressed in this fashion—read, sip, baste, read, sip, baste. Did I mention I was enjoying some well-chilled Gruet? When the chicken was so tender that the wings were about to take flight *sans* the body, I put the roasting pan on the counter and tented it with parchment.

The aroma had Geronimo howling. After the chicken had

cooled enough to handle, I took the meat off the back, legs and wings and gave it to him. He stared at the plump breasts as if comparing our portions.

"This is mine," I told him. He slinked away.

If Dolly had joined me for dinner, I would have prepared a side or two, perhaps a salad as well. But as it was just us guys, we both ate a politically incorrect all-meat supper. I finished the bottle of Gruet and had enough judgment left to ignore the little voice urging me to open a second one.

30

Which was a good idea because I needed my wits about me Sunday morning when Whit Fletcher and Danny Duran showed up at my door looking like the before and after pictures for a fitness center, Duran's muscles bulging under a leather jacket, Fletcher's paunch draped with his trademark shiny one-size-too-large silver suit.

Detective First Grade Whit Fletcher of the Albuquerque Police Department is a friend or nemesis. Maybe both. He has no interest in enforcing the Archaeological Resources Protection Act, reasoning that if there's money to be made by selling old pots and no one gets hurt, what's the problem? That's also his view about cops making a little something on the side. He would never take a bribe, but if there's money no one is going to miss, it generally winds up in his pocket.

I've expedited his little bonuses by doing things like selling a pot after it was used as evidence in a trial and no one claimed ownership. Like a pot in the ground, he figures one in the evidence locker serves its best and highest use by being converted to cash.

He in turn has helped me out of a few scrapes with the police, although I can't give him full credit because he got me into some of them in the first place.

None of my mental pigeon-holes would accept Fletcher and Duran together at my front door, so I just stared at them uncomprehendingly.

Whit said, "Good morning, Hubert."

My head swung left and right as I kept looking at them in turn thinking one of them would turn out to be an apparition.

"Be better if you invited us in," said Whit. "You wouldn't want that dame two doors down eavesdropping on our conversation."

"Miss Gladys is too much a lady to eavesdrop," I said as I stepped out of the door and allowed them to enter.

"You got any coffee?" Whit asked. I shook my head.

"Seeing as how you're not fully awake, why don't I get us some?"

I thought that was a good idea. Maybe I could get my brain in gear while he was going for the coffee. But he walked back to the kitchen and hit the brew button on my coffeemaker.

Whit plopped down in my papasan chair, and I took one of the harder kitchen ones. Duran remained standing.

"Detective Duran called me to say he was thinking about hauling you in for more questioning. The coroner suspects Barry Stiles didn't die of natural causes. We had a long talk, and I convinced Danny to come down on a day off and let the three of us see if we can't handle this thing sort of unofficial for now."

Duran took out his notebook. He unwrapped a piece of gum and stuck it in his mouth. "I want a rundown of your whereabouts on Sunday night and Monday of last week, starting with when you woke up and ending with when you went to sleep."

Ah. So Susannah was right when she said I'd be a suspect in

the murder of Barry Stiles, although I thought I remembered her reasoning was all based on Bernie Rhodenbarr. Maybe Duran read those books, too.

After taking a few seconds to organize my thoughts, I said, "I spent Sunday night here."

"Can anyone verify that?"

"Yes. I had a guest that evening."

"Would that be your Mexican girlfriend with the big hooters?" asked Whit.

I ignored him. Duran shook his head slightly.

"And the next morning?"

"I left shortly after ten and drove to *Schnitzel*. I got there about eleven thirty. They called everyone to lunch around noon. I went to the dining area and learned the lunch was *Schokogugelhupf*, so I didn't stay."

"Where did you go?"

"Wait a minute," said Whit. "What was lunch?"

"*Schokogugelhupf.*"

"That's what I thought you said. What the hell is showgogugel-hump?"

"Some kind of cake."

"Why don't they just say so?"

I shrugged.

Duran repeated his question. "Where did you go?"

"I went back to my work area. They were letting me do my work in the private dining room."

"You didn't leave the building?"

"No."

"Then what?"

"After lunch, Alain Billot came to talk to me. Then I went to dinner. It was fried carp, so I skipped that, too."

Fletcher said, "Ain't healthy skipping meals, Hubert."

"Oh, I forgot. Billot brought me a *croque monsieur*."

"Is that French for a dead guy?"

"A *croque monsieur* is a sandwich."

"Then why don't they just call it that?"

Duran looked impatient. "What happened after that?"

"I drove to the hotel with Jürgen Dorfmeister, and we spent the rest of the evening in the bar downstairs."

"When was the last time you saw Barry Stiles?"

"I can't say for sure. He was at the restaurant on Monday. I saw everybody at some point. They move around a lot."

"Can the others verify that you never left the restaurant from the time you arrived until you left with Dorfmeister?"

"I think so."

"You *think* so?"

"I didn't have a constant escort. But the door to my area is open and people are walking by all the time. It's unlikely I could leave the building without being seen."

The coffee was ready. I let Whit pour it because I was sitting on my hands so they wouldn't shake.

"When did Dorfmeister leave?"

"Around midnight."

"Where did he go?"

I knew he would get to this part, so I had tried to think in advance what I would say. "I don't know. He asked for the keys to my Bronco. I told him he was too drunk to drive, but he said he was going to sleep in it."

"Did he?"

"I didn't go down to see."

"Why didn't you tell me this on Tuesday?"

"You didn't ask."

Duran worked the gum. *Chomp. Chomp.*

"Besides," I added, "I didn't think it was relevant."

"I'll be the judge of that. What happened next?"

"I told you. I went to the parking garage the next morning and found Barry Stiles dead in the back of my truck."

"Oh, come on, Detective," said Whit, "Tell him what you told me. Hubert here will play straight with you. I can vouch for that."

Duran rolled his eyes ever so slightly. "I think the reason you didn't tell me is—"

At this point I was sure the next words out of his mouth would be, "because you killed Barry Stiles."

But they were, "because you were trying to protect Jürgen Dorfmeister."

"No. That never even occurred to me."

"Come on, Schuze. If you're really going to play it straight with me like Detective Fletcher says, tell me what the first thought was that crossed your mind when you saw that body in your truck."

"I thought Jürgen had lost eighty pounds."

"What!" Duran looked at Fletcher. "This is the guy you say will play it straight with me?"

"I was groggy. You wanted my first thought. That was it. I realized in just a couple of seconds that it was ridiculous, but that was my first thought."

Fletcher started laughing. "You don't think he would make that up, do you?"

"Nobody thinks like that," said Duran.

"Nobody *normal*. But Hubert here don't think like you and me. He once told me he could prove he hadn't been at a murder site because he was somewhere else alone."

That wasn't exactly right, but it was close, and I didn't want to argue because Whit was trying to help even though he was making me out to be an idiot in the process.

Evidently, Duran wasn't buying my story. "I questioned everyone at the restaurant. Seems they don't get along too well. Dorfmeister is one of two people we know had access to where the body was found. The other one is you. You're not part of the restaurant crowd, and so far everyone backs up your story that you and Stiles barely knew each other. So Dorfmeister is our best bet. You two spent a night together at the bar. Two guys at a bar for hours drinking, they tell each other things. He told you something, maybe that he and Stiles had a run-in. When Stiles showed up dead, you were afraid Dorfmeister did it, and that's why you didn't mention him when I first questioned you."

"No. I didn't suspect Jürgen or anyone else because there was nothing to suspect anyone of. I didn't even know Barry had been murdered until you mentioned it this morning," I said, looking at Whit. "And on top of that," I added, "Jürgen never mentioned Barry that night."

Duran jumped on that. "When *did* he mention him?"

"Tuesday night. We were at the bar again and he proposed a toast—'To the memory of Mr. Barry Stiles, *garde manger extraordinaire*'."

"What the hell does 'guard man-jay extraordinary' mean?" asked Whit.

"Think about it, Schuze," said Duran. "Try to remember something else Dorfmeister may have said about Stiles. You and I will be talking again."

31

I took Geronimo for a long walk after Fletcher and Duran left. He seemed to sense I was worried because instead of sniffing everything along the way, he kept looking back at me as if checking on my mood.

I couldn't shake the feeling that Duran had threatened me. If I didn't come up with something to implicate Jürgen, Danny boy was going to elevate me to chief suspect. It crossed my mind that he wanted me to fabricate something if nothing was there. I put that thought aside.

I called Susannah because I needed to talk to someone. When she heard the subject, she said it was too important to deal with over the phone.

Dos Hermanas was closed, so we agreed she would come to my place. I made the simple version of *guacamole*—smash the avocados with a fork and add salsa. I put two beer glasses in the freezer because it was too early for margaritas.

When she arrived, I told her about my conversation with Fletcher and Duran.

Just as I finished, Martin showed up. I had only two glasses in the freezer, but that didn't matter. He likes his Tecate straight from the can.

We sat at my kitchen table, warmed by the strong New Mexico sun that had the room around eighty even though it was in the forties outside.

Susannah brought Martin up to date. She grabbed a large chip and used it like a professor might use an eraser, jabbing it in my direction to make a point. "Here's how I think it went down. Dorfmeister and Stiles were lovers. When Jürgen found himself alone in the Bronco, he called Stiles. They had a lover's quarrel, and Jürgen killed him."

"That's ridiculous. Jürgen isn't gay."

"You didn't think Chris was gay either until he kissed you."

Martin started laughing. "I miss something?"

"Susannah asked me to help a former boyfriend with his English, and during one of the lessons, he kissed me."

"On the mouth?"

"Can we get back to Dorfmeister, please?"

"Okay," she said. "He went out of his way to make your acquaintance and invited himself to your bar twice."

"I'll concede he might be gay, although I still doubt it. But how did he kill Stiles? There was no blood."

"He choked him to death."

"I saw his neck. There were no bruises."

"He smothered him."

I shook my head. "Jürgen is an out of shape guy in his fifties. Barry was a lean fit guy about your age. There is no way that could happen."

"He injected him with poison."

"Right. He found himself in the back of my Bronco and arranged an impromptu tryst in a parking garage when the temperature was in the forties. Then when he and Barry had a lovers' spat, Jürgen just happened to have a hypodermic needle and some poison."

"It may sound ridiculous, Hubert, but you already said Duran believes Dorfmeister did it. And it's a lot more likely than your theory that the murderer just happened to throw his victim in your truck because the window was down."

"Hearing about restaurants and parking garages makes me appreciate the reservation," said Martin. He opened the door and let Geronimo in. Susannah rubbed him behind the ears. Geronimo, that is.

I said, "Raoul Deschutes thinks Kuchen may have killed Barry." She finally stuck the pointer chip in the dip and ate it. "Why?"

"He didn't say, but it makes more sense than anything the two of us have come up with. Barry told me he was going to get revenge on Kuchen by getting him fired. Maybe Kuchen knew that and decided to kill Barry before it happened."

"How could Barry get Kuchen fired?"

"I have no idea. All I know is he said to me, 'I know something no one else here knows'."

Susannah was now fully immersed in her Girl Detective mode. She's told me many times how much she enjoyed reading the Nancy Drew books when she was of that age. I've also read that Sonia Sotomayor, Hillary Clinton, and Laura Bush cited them as formative influences. If there's a common denominator among those four women, I can't find it.

"Since *Schnitzel* is so new," she said, "it must be something about Kuchen's past. Barry and he must have crossed paths at a previous restaurant. Maybe Café Alsace?"

"No, Kuchen wasn't at Alsace because when I introduced Rafael to him, it was clear they had never met."

"You got a pad and pencil?" asked Martin. "I think I need a score card to keep up with this."

Susannah asked, "You know where Kuchen's last job was?"

"I got the impression he came straight from Europe. Maybe he worked at *Le Petit Moulin Rouge*." The name of the place had stuck in my mind.

She gave me a strange look. "The place where Toulouse-Lautrec hung out?"

"I don't know. Evidently, it's a famous restaurant in Paris. Or used to be. Escoffier worked there."

"When did Escoffier live?"

"1846 to 1935."

"Toulouse-Lautrec was commissioned to do posters for *Moulin Rouge* in 1889, so they might have overlapped." When she's not waiting tables at *La Placita*, Susannah studies art history as a part-time night student at the University of New Mexico.

"Did you ever see the movie *Moulin Rouge*?" I asked her.

"Sure. And I watched it again when I took up art history. They didn't have computer animation back then so they had to use clever staging and camera angles to make José Ferrer look like he was four foot six."

"I remember Zsa Zsa Gabor played the model."

"She was actually a dancer at *Moulin Rouge*," said Susannah.

"I know she's real old," I said, "but I don't think Zsa Zsa Gabor was alive in 1889."

"Of course not. The dancer was named Jane Avril. When they hired Lautrec to make posters for the business, he selected Avril as his model. Why are we talking about this?"

"Because you asked me where Kuchen last worked, and I said maybe at *Le Petit Moulin Rouge*."

"Oh, right. I don't think they're the same place. You said *Le Petit Moulin Rouge* was a famous restaurant. *Moulin Rouge* was mainly a bar and dance hall. From what you've told me about Escoffier, I don't think he would have worked there."

"I'm glad we got that cleared up," quipped Martin. "You got any more beer?"

We were all ready for a second one, so I pulled three from the fridge.

"The *guacamole* is all gone," observed Martin.

"We still have chips."

"You want us to eat plain chips?" asked Susannah.

"Why is it I have to provide the food every time we get together?"

Susannah said, "I could provide some *pintxos* next time."

"Which are?"

"Bar food. One of my favorites is *txipirones*."

"How do you spell that," I said because I knew she wanted me to. She smiled. "Just like it sounds."

"And what is it?" asked Martin

"Squid cooked in its own ink."

Martin looked at me. "You try it first, paleface."

"What will you bring?" I asked him.

"*Pih-n.*"

"Which is?"

"Gopher."

"I'll make some salsa," I said.

32

I spent five hours making *mole* after Susannah and Martin left.

Despite the spelling, it is unrelated to the gopher.

I placed the gigantic pot from *Schnitzel* on my stove where it covered both burners and began filling it with ingredients. Most of them had to be processed in some way before being tossed into the mix, which accounts for the five hours.

The sesame seeds, dried *ancho chiles*, almonds, anise seeds, *cominos*, and *pepitas* had to be dry-roasted in a frying pan in separate batches, shaking the pan constantly as if making popcorn. The tomatillos and garlic had to be chopped. The Mexican *canela*, black pepper and fresh cloves had to be ground. The Mexican chocolate needed to be roughly chopped.

A few pieces of the chocolate didn't make it into the pot.

The bread had to be toasted. The chicken broth had to be made from scratch. Only the corn oil and my secret substitute ingredient—black cherries instead of raisins—went into the pot without being processed.

After the brew was simmering, I popped the cork on a bottle of Gruet which I told myself I had earned by hard labor. Ella Fitzgerald was singing *Baby It's Cold Outside*, and the scent from the *mole* had my taste buds doing a slow rumba. Only my iron will and the cold Gruet kept me from eating some of the *mole* before it was completely done. About halfway to that point, I dropped in five dozen chicken legs.

I never cook in large batches, so I had no idea how long it would take. I fished out one of the legs after a while, put it on my cutting board and pressed it. From the way it sprung back, I thought it might be done. I cut into it. It was.

I didn't want to put it back in the pot after handling it and cutting into it. That was the excuse I gave myself for eating it. Then I had to test several more.

The ones I didn't eat went onto the cookie sheets. I covered them with foil and slid them into the fridge.

As an experiment, I mixed Geronimo's dry dog food with some *mole*. He liked it.

33

Molinero had generously allowed me to keep my room at *La Fonda* until the plates were finished. I thought the least I could do was be there to help with the Grand Opening.

They pressed me into service as a *garçon de cuisine*. Also known as a kitchen boy.

I didn't mind. They needed the help.

I showed up at ten in the morning thinking I was absurdly early only to find the kitchen in tumult. Masoot was baking bread, Scruggs' assistants were hauling pots and pans to the scullery the moment they were emptied, Mansfield was filling various plastic containers on a shelf over his station, Mure was frenching racks of lamb, Salazar had various sauces in process and Billot was trussing up some chickens.

"*Regarde*," he said when he saw me watching, "They are all tied up with a knot."

I smiled. "The expression is 'tied up with a bow'."

"Ah. Well, I have used the knot."

Luckily for the chickens, they were dead—being tied in that position looked very uncomfortable.

Rafael was making *pâté* and Raoul was removing filets from a large fish and putting what was left in a pot to make fish stock. Jürgen was carving a large piece of beef into pieces that would become *tafelspitz*, which is as unappetizing as the name would suggest. Kuchen was going from station to station making comments and issuing orders.

When I said I was willing to help, they didn't hesitate to accept. Despite the weeks of preparation, many things had been overlooked. No one had thought to start storing ice, so all they had was what the machine held. They sent me on an ice run. I filled the back of the Bronco and Scruggs helped me carry the bags to the freezer when I returned.

I folded napkins and filled salt shakers.

Among all the ranks of the *brigade de cuisine* mentioned in Escoffier's book, the only one missing was the *communard*, the person who prepares meals for the staff. I had intended for my chicken *mole* to be merely a treat and a thank-you for the staff on their big day, but Alain made a pot of rice to go with it, and it became the staff lunch. There was no time for one of the group lunches we had during training and no place either since the dining room was now fully dressed in its finest linen and silver. People took a leg and some rice and ate standing up or moving.

I worked until five when they told me to stand aside because they had a routine for the hour before opening.

Wallace Voile had a cadre of lithe young women serving as hostesses and waitresses, and she was giving them last minute instructions. Her crew were dressed in black skirts and simple white blouses with red ascots. Wallace wore a silver-sequined dress that clung to her contours, starting from her neck, flaring slightly at the knees, continuing down to the floor and trailing her as she walked. Rafael walked up to me and said, "Wow! Get a load of that body."

"That dress makes her look like a mermaid," I said.

"Yeah. Thirty-six, twenty four, carp."

Kuchen came out in a freshly washed and pressed tunic. The tables were set, the lights were lowered. The castle gates were thrown open.

The obvious chaos of the last eight hours gave way to casual competence in the dining room. In the kitchen, pandemonium continued to reign, but it was a controlled hubbub. Backstage at an opera, the costumes and sets so obviously counterfeit, the faces of the singers painted on. Yet the audience sees only glorious spectacle.

Food was dropped, plates broken, curses uttered. But when the swinging door opened and the waiters arrived with the dishes, it seemed effortless to the diners.

The tables were packed all night. Wine flowed, coffers filled. When the door was locked behind the last patron, champagne was uncorked—not Gruet, alas—and toasts were made. To Kuchen, to Molinero, to the staff, to Santa Fe, to food and to success, which seemed to me the most appropriate toast of all because that is what the Grand Opening had been—an overwhelming success.

I walked back to *La Fonda*. When I entered the lobby, I was surprised a round of applause did not break out. I felt the whole world must surely know about *Schnitzel*, and I was proud to be a part of it.

34

The euphoria evaporated over morning coffee at the French Café. The headline on the review by Dagmar Mortensen, the restaurant critic for the state's major paper read, "A *Herr* in my Soup." The text was about what you would expect given the headline.

Many of us were looking forward to a new cuisine in town. After all, Austrian restaurants are as rare in New Mexico as a rainy day. After dining at *Schnitzel* last night, I now understand why. The evening began well. The entry to *Schnitzel* looks like Mad King Ludwig's Bavarian Castle. The *maitresse d'* was welcoming and lovely in her shimmering dress. Our table setting was impressive. Everything went well until the food arrived.

I started with the coachman's salad, constructed from bologna, hard-boiled eggs, cucumber, and onions sliced in Cobb salad style. The dressing was a fatty mayonnaise concoction.

The bologna, onion, and mayo created a taste you would expect from a county fair kiosk sponsored by Oscar Meyer and Kraft.

The fingerling potatoes in my companion's warm potato salad were overcooked and oily. The only things required to turn our first course into the picnic from hell would have been ants and rain.

The entrées were worse. My *Gebratener Leberkäse* contained two rich meats, corned beef and bacon. I don't know which was worse, the cloying flavor or the existential angst about which part of my anatomy the fat was going to disfigure. My companion, having taken the warning shot of her salad seriously, tried to play it safe by ordering chicken strudel, something that sounds both traditionally Austrian and light by comparison to my meatloaf. Her hopes were dashed when the chicken arrived.

At least we assumed there was chicken in there. The salty ham and heavy layer of cheese hid the bird well. Just to make sure no chicken taste would peek through, sour cream had been liberally applied.

I almost decided to skip dessert, which would have been a mistake. The *Salzburger Nockerln* and *Linzer torte* were good, although not good enough to justify eating what had come before.

Judging from *Schnitzel*, Austrian food will not be a hit in the Land of Enchantment. It is too dark for this sunny clime. Because it relies so heavily on fat, sugar and salt, it has a tired formulaic taste one might expect in the cafeteria of a tourist boat on the Danube. After it sank. I have decided to make *Schnitzel* the first restaurant I have ever awarded minus two stars.

My mood had darkened with every word. My coffee had also grown cooler because I was too engrossed to drink it. I was mortified for my colleagues, especially Rafael. I had urged him to become the *garde manger* at *Schnitzel*, and now his two salads had been viciously panned in the state's leading paper.

I picked up a daily from Albuquerque and warily turned each page the way a bomb defuser might remove sand from around a land mine. There was no mention of *Schnitzel*. Then I saw the second section. Above the fold in large print, I read, "Austrians probably glad *Schnitzel* chef immigrated." The review began, "Historians looking for an explanation of the fall of the Austro-Hungarian Empire might want to start with the food." I couldn't read any further.

But that didn't stop me from checking another Santa Fe paper where I found this gem of a headline—"Lederhosen tastier than meatloaf at *Schnitzel*." I decided to run away from the mess. Get in the Bronco, drive back to Albuquerque and take the phone off the hook. Then I reconsidered.

There was no reason to take the phone of the hook. No one was going to call me about *Schnitzel*. I was just the 'ceramic artist'.

But even though they were an odd lot to say the least, I knew I couldn't abandon the people at *Schnitzel* in what had to be the nadir of their professional careers.

Then I saw one of them walk into the café. Smiling, of all things.

"I thought I might find you here," said Jürgen as he sat down. He eyed the table. "You have already eaten?"

"No, but I've lost my appetite."

"Ach!" he scoffed. He went to the counter and purchased two almond croissants and two fresh coffees.

I sipped the hot coffee and felt a little better. I risked a bite of the croissant. It was warm, flaky, and sweet. I had another bite and some more coffee.

"You're not depressed by the reviews?"

He waved a hand dismissively, "If we gave the newspapers bad reviews would people stop reading them?"

"I guess not."

"Just so. People do not stop going to restaurants that get bad reviews. Anyway, restaurant reviews are for snobs."

Evidently I had a lot to learn. Jürgen's words of experience and even keel made me feel better. I stopped worrying about *Schnitzel*.

And returned to worrying about Detective Duran.

I looked around to ascertain no one was sitting next to us. I lowered my voice. "Jürgen, are you gay?"

"Of course! You will never see me in a bad mood. Since I left home on my sixteenth birthday, I have traveled the world as what you Americans call a happy-go-lucky man."

I cleared my throat. "That's not what I meant. I mean are you a . . ."

"Homosexual?" he said when I hesitated. "Why do you ask? Do you wish to proposition me?"

"I'm not gay. But someone I know thinks you might be."

This was not going at all as I intended. I felt like an idiot for bringing it up.

He looked amused. "And why does this person you know speculate about me in this fashion?"

I didn't know whether I was supposed to do so, but I decided to tell him about my second meeting with Duran. "Detective Duran thinks you may have killed Barry Stiles."

He looked puzzled. "And he thinks I did this because I am gay?"

"No, he doesn't think you're gay. At least I don't *think* he does. I'm not sure."

"Then I do not understand."

Neither did I, and I was the one doing the explaining. "Duran says only two people had obvious access to where the body was found, you and me. Since I didn't really know Barry, Duran assumes I had no reason to kill him."

"But I didn't know him any better than you did."

"I know. But because you are both cooks, he thinks there might be a connection."

"He thinks cooks are gay?"

"No. I was talking to a friend about it, and she was trying to help me by figuring out how Barry was killed. So she said one possibility is that when you went to the Bronco, you called him to meet you there."

"And I would do that because I am gay?"

"I told her it was a ridiculous idea."

"I am not gay," he stated matter of factly. "I have never wanted to be tied down by marriage. Perhaps I saw how much my mother needed marriage, and I didn't want to be so dependent. I enjoy sex with women, but as Machlin said to me when we were discussing the subject, he loves bread, but he doesn't want to own a bakery."

Oink, I said to myself since Susannah wasn't there to say it.

35

The bedlam at *Schnitzel* Tuesday night was the same as it had been at the Grand Opening, and I was again assigned a number of unskilled tasks that no one else had time to do. I removed wax drippings from candle holders, made a trip to Whole Foods for fennel bulbs and wrote the specials on a slate board next to the *maitresse d'* station.

Most places use a white board these days, but *Schnitzel* had real slate. Alain Billot gave me the list, and I used my best printing to list the items.

In addition to the set menu, there was to be a special appetizer, entrée, and dessert—smoked trout *pâté*, *beuschel* and *Apfelstrudel* respectively.

You know what *Apfelstrudel* is. You don't want to know what *beuschel* is, but I'm going to tell you anyway—a ragout with calf lungs and heart. Yum.

I had Jürgen proofread the list because I assumed Alain was not fluent in Austrian. I say 'Austrian' because when I had called it German, Kuchen told me in no uncertain terms it was Austrian. There are evidently a few differences in spelling and usage as there are in English between the U.S. and England, but Kuchen took them seriously, pointing out that whereas Germans write the word for 'foot' as 'fuß', Austrians write is as 'fuss'.

I immediately took the Austrian side of this weighty issue, having investigated the dreaded ß—called an *eszett* I now knew—after Susannah drew one for me when explaining about it being on the uniforms of some Nazis. I found a book in the library about scripts around the world. I had decided I didn't like it. The *eszett*, that is. I liked the book fine, but didn't mention it to Susannah for fear of the scolding she would give me for reading something which has neither practical application nor entertainment value.

I made a tour of the restaurant during the few minutes immediately before opening and no one seemed worried. Perhaps they were too busy to worry. Everything was the same as it had been the night before with the exception of Kuchen who was nowhere to be seen. Molinero was also not there. His office was dark and I assumed locked.

There was a line when the doors opened, and most of the tables had diners until eight when the crowd began to thin. The last patrons left shortly after ten, and it was after midnight when the lights were turned out and the doors locked.

I was halfway down the block when Jürgen caught up with me and suggested we hit the bar. I told him I was too tired. I also told him he was right that people would come to *Schnitzel* despite the bad reviews. Then, remembering that P.T. Barnum is reputed to have said, "Say anything you want about me as long as you spell my name right," I said to Jürgen that perhaps the people came *because* of the bad reviews.

During this brief exchange, Rafael Pacheco walked by with Wallace Voile clinging to his arm. Deschutes was about twenty feet back, seemingly following them. Next came Maria Salazar and Helen Mure. Maria smiled at me as she passed by. Helen stared straight ahead.

I fell in behind the strange parade and headed to *La Fonda*.

36

On Wednesday morning, I put my dirty clothes behind the back seat and headed home. And thought again about Barry Stiles.

Joseph Akerman was born in Wiltshire, England, not far from Southampton where the *Titanic* embarked. He joined her crew as a pantryman on April 4, 1912. I suppose a pantryman is something like a *garde manger*. His wages were £3 15s per month. Before I returned to school to study something of interest, I earned an accounting degree at UNM, but they didn't teach us how to convert pounds and schillings to dollars. £3 15s doesn't sound like much, but perhaps a hundred years ago it was a living wage. Akerman never got to find out. He died in the sinking, as did his brother, Albert, who was a steward.

Joseph and Albert Akerman were immortalized in a small way by having their pictures and obituaries published in Escoffier's magazine. They are also on the list of the fifteen hundred people who died with them in the cold waters of the North Atlantic. I suppose most people who die are listed somewhere, but the *Titanic* is an A-list. People are fascinated by the story.

Dying while an employee of *Schnitzel* hardly ranks up there with dying as a crewmember of the *Titanic*, but Stiles was just as dead as Akerman. He just wouldn't be on an A-list of the deceased. Did it matter? I didn't think so.

These morose thoughts faded as I approached Old Town. After parking and unloading, I strolled over to the plaza. The air was crisp and the sun warm. The hodgepodge of adobe walls, wrought iron benches and gallerias with their dried and splitting carved posts and lintels dispatched the last of my gloomy thoughts.

Live in the moment. If the moment finds you in a charmed place, all the better.

Geronimo was happy to see me. I'd had left him plenty of food and water, and he had left me a few things in the patio that I scooped up and deposited in the trash.

The luster of my simple home had faded somewhat due to my running back and forth to Santa Fe, so I spent the day doing house-work and laundry. The loud bong noise activated by the opening of the front door would alert me to customers. It bonged twice but the people who triggered it did not stay long. My straightening, dust-ing, waxing and washing were done by four-fifty. And even had they not been, I would have left for *Dos Hermanas* at any rate.

After the margaritas were served, I was disappointed to hear she hadn't seen the reviews because that meant the task of telling her Rafael's salads were flamed by the critics now fell to me.

"The reviews were bad," I said.

"How bad?"

"Very bad."

"Very bad or very, very bad?"

"Even worse."

"What's worse than very, very bad?"

"How about Dagmar Mortensen saying the coachman's salad tasted like something from a county fair kiosk sponsored by Oscar Meyer and Kraft."

Her eyes narrowed. "What else?"

"She said her companion's warm potato salad was overcooked and oily."

"Anything else?" she asked through clenched jaws.

Might as well get it all out. "There was something along the lines of the only things required to turn the salad course into the picnic from hell would have been ants and rain."

"I want her to review *La Placita*, Hubert."

"Why? She delights in being negative."

"Yeah? Well here's a line for her—'My enchiladas were laced with coyote poison from a ranch in Willard and I'm—hack, gag, choke—feeling too weak to finish this review'."

"Look at the bright side. She didn't mention his name."

"I hate that woman, Hubert. How is Ice taking it?"

I thought of him the night after the reviews, smiling as he walking along with Wallace Voile clinging to his arm. "It doesn't seem to be bothering him," I said with a straight face.

"Just being brave on the outside, I bet."

"Maybe you should call him."

"He's at work and won't get off until close to midnight."

I thought for a while. "The first time you mentioned him to me was only a few weeks ago, and he's been in Santa Fe for almost half of the time since."

"And your point is?"

I didn't know what my point was. I was seeking an oblique entry into murky waters. "It's none of my business, but if I had a girl-friend in Albuquerque, I wouldn't mind her calling me in Santa Fe late at night."

"You *did* have a girlfriend in Albuquerque when you were in Santa Fe. Did Dolly ever call you after midnight?"

"Yes."

"Oh." She picked up a chip and held it above the salsa absent-mindedly. After an awkward silence, she said, "Are you trying to tell me something?"

"No," I said a little too emphatically. "I'm just saying that if you feel close enough to call him late, he might appreciate it."

"Why? You said the bad review didn't seem to bother him."

"And you said he was just being brave on the outside."

Another awkward silence. The chip was still poised above the salsa like a reluctant diver on the end of the high board.

"What made you think he's taking it well?" she finally asked.

"He seemed happy the night after the reviews."

She started to say something but changed her mind. Then she ate the chip, smiled and said, "Is there a way out of this conversa-tion?"

"Thank you. Ask me about something else."

"Okay. Have you resolved your dilemma about how to shop for a wife while you're going steady with Dolly?"

I wished again I had never used that phrase. "I'm not going steady with her."

"Maybe you didn't give her your high school ring, but if you won't date anyone else, then that's going steady."

"I didn't buy a high school ring."

She ignored that. "What does Dolly say about your relationship?"

I wondered why Susannah has no qualms about discussing

my relationships, and I get a nervous stomach when trying to talk about hers.

"She never talks about it."

Her eyes dilated. "She's never said something, like 'Where do you see this going?' or 'I wish we could spend more time together', something like that?"

"Nope."

"You've been dating for four months and even sleeping together and she's never mentioned your relationship?"

I shook my head.

"How is that possible? Don't you talk about arrangements or something?"

"I invite her over sometimes. She invites me over sometimes. We talk on the phone now and then."

"What do you say to each other at the end of a date?"

"Goodnight. I had a great time. Things like that."

"The woman is strange, Hubie."

I shrugged. "Maybe it's an age thing. She's settled, independent. She has a home. She evidently doesn't need money because she doesn't work."

"Probably gets tons of alimony."

"Meow."

"I deserved that." She laughed. "So you're saying she doesn't want a normal relationship with you. She's perfectly happy to go to your place, have a great meal and a roll in the hay, and then go home."

I smiled my boyish smile. "Wham, bam, thank you ma'am."

She shook her head. "Every man's dream."

37

I picked up Dolly on Thursday morning, and we drove down the old road towards the Isleta Pueblo. It was a typical New Mexico winter day, cold dry air and bright sunshine. The trees were bare and the lawns yellow. The grass crunched beneath my feet.

"Who is this Consuela we're going to see?"

"My second mother."

"Your father remarried after your mother died?"

The thought of my father being married to Consuela made me chuckle. "No, she was my nanny, although I don't think I ever heard that word until I was in high school. But that's what she was. She took care of me from the time my mother brought me home from the hospital."

"Your mother worked?"

"No, but she was involved in a lot of activities."

"I didn't think university professors made enough money to have nannies for their kids."

"I never thought about it. It seemed we had everything we needed, but we lived modestly. A small house near the university, a Chevy which my mother usually drove. My dad walked to work. I don't think they paid Consuela much. She was an immigrant, happy to be in the U.S., and they supplied room and board, so she was able to save most of what she earned."

"Don't mention it to my dad. You'll have to endure another lecture on immigration issues."

Frank Aguirre was the first faculty member at Albuquerque High School to get a Ph.D., and he wrote his dissertation on immigration policy.

"I like talking to your father about immigration."

"The history of it in the nineteenth century?"

"That can be a little dull, but when he gets into the contemporary issues, it's fascinating."

"To you maybe. I was glad to get away today. I've heard more about the new Arizona Immigration Law than I can stand."

"Maybe you need to develop more of a sense of Yuma."

I was the only one who laughed.

Emilio spotted us when we turned off the highway and was standing out in the cold to greet me with a warm *abrazo*. He bowed when I introduced Dolly, and we went in to see Consuela who was standing by her favorite chair with her hand on its back for support. The house smelled freshly cleaned.

Dolly's brown sugar skin and the last name Aguirre prompted Consuela to welcome her in Spanish and tell her how happy she was that I had brought my girlfriend to meet them.

I couldn't tell whether Dolly's blush was because she didn't speak Spanish or because she recognized the word *novia*.

"*Lo siento. Yo no hablo español,*" said Dolly.

"If you want to learn, Consuela is a great teacher," I said as I hugged her.

We made small talk until Emilio said he needed my help with the *barbacoa*. When we got to the back patio he said he just wanted to leave the women alone to chat. Just what I need, I thought. Oh well, they had to meet sooner or later. I could only hope Consuela wouldn't quiz Dolly about whether she wanted to have children.

Emilio and I went for a walk along the irrigation canal towards the river. "She grows weak, *Uberto*."

"I know. Perhaps she will need a transplant."

"What she wants is for Ninfa to return home and have a child."

I nodded. We walked on in silence.

"*Tengo una pregunta, pero quizás no es apropiada.*"

Emilio often switches to Spanish when he thinks the topic is serious.

I told him in Spanish that nothing he could ask would be inappropriate. After some hesitation, he asked me how I felt about the fact that my parents had died before I had children.

By this time we were approaching the *bosque*, so we turned back east.

"My father was a man of abstract ideas. My mother was a social activist. They were good parents, Emilio, but your wife raised me. I don't remember my father or my mother ever discussing grandchildren."

"But they have you, *Uberto*. And Consuela and I have Ninfa. We must all leave a child for the world. Is it not so?"

I thought about it as we walked along in silence. My parents had a happy marriage. But would it have been less felicitous had I never been born? Miss Gladys had a long and presumably happy marriage to Guy Claiborne. Would not having children have changed that? Susannah's mother obviously regarded the single life as a step or two down from death and dismemberment. Even the confused runaway Kaylee who had shown up on my doorstep eventually married her fellow potscrubber, Arturo, and the two of them were having a child they probably couldn't afford. Bees do it. Even educated fleas do it.

Would Dolly and I join the insect world and procreate? Was it too late for that?

I have a series of theses I call Schuze's Anthropological Premises or SAP, which is what my cynical friends say you have to be to believe them.

My SAPs deal with evolution, culture, ethnicity and a host of other related issues. Oddly, none of them deal with marriage and children. If I ever have any insight on those topics, perhaps I'll add a new SAP to the list.

We took the meat inside. A lace tablecloth I had never seen was under the plates. A vase of flowers sat where the salt and pepper normally resided. We had a pleasant but somewhat formal lunch.

As we left, Consuela said to me in Spanish that she thought Dolly would be a wonderful wife and she was honored I brought her to meet them. I kissed her goodbye but made no reply to the wife comment.

Dolly gave me a sly smile once we were on the road. "Are you going to tell me what Consuela said as we were leaving?"

"She said you look sexually frustrated and told me I should do something about it as soon as possible."

She hit me with her left arm.

"You didn't understand any of it?"

"You know I don't speak Spanish. The only thing I know how to say is 'I don't speak Spanish', and I learned that only because it comes up so often."

"I thought maybe you caught the word *novia* when we first arrived."

"Yeah. I know a few other common words that everyone in Albuquerque knows because you hear them so often. One of those common words is *esposa*. It was the only word I picked up there at the end."

"You want to know what she said?"

"Yes."

"She said you would make a wonderful wife."

The twenty seconds of silence that followed took about ten minutes.

"This is awkward, Hubie."

Another twenty second of silence. A few more and we'd be back in town. She looked out through the windshield. "I don't know what your thoughts are on the subject of marriage. It hasn't worked for me in the past, so I decided I wouldn't try it again. I don't presume you would ask me or not ask me, but—"

"I—"

"Let me finish. I like my life. I enjoy my independence. I enjoy decorating the house and having it look just the way I want. I have my dad to look after, but I enjoy that, and he's never demanding. He's good company when I want it and he keeps to his books when I don't. I like to cook. I like to garden. In short, I'm content."

She turned to look at me. "When you knocked on my door, romance came back into my life. Now my life is even better. I might even say complete. I like the way things are now. I'd like to keep it that way."

I let that soak in for a while. "So what now?"

"I hope we continue to see each other. I'm too content to be the jealous type. What you do when we're not together is none of my business."

"I meant now as in *now*, this afternoon."

She smiled at me. "I thought that was obvious. We go to your place and see what you can do about that sexual frustration Consuela says I have."

38

I stopped by Feats of Clay a few days later and discovered their kiln master was out sick, and they were as badly behind schedule on my plates as the Highway Department is on the widening of Interstate 25. Since they weren't receiving tax money, I decided to forgive them.

Only half the plates had been formed, and none of the edelweiss overlays had been cut. The glazing was merely a vague intention.

I felt bad again for the delay. I felt even worse when Alain Billot called me at eleven at night on the next Saturday and asked me to attend an emergency meeting of the staff of *Schnitzel* the next afternoon.

When I asked what the emergency was, he said he didn't want to talk about it on the phone. I told him I didn't want to make another trip to Santa Fe, but when he said it was important for me to be there, I relented.

When I arrived, Billot scooted me into the bar. "Kuchen has not been seen since the grand opening."

"I noticed he wasn't there the next night, but I figured maybe he was sick."

He smiled. "You thought perhaps he had the bad review disease?"

"Well, yes."

"It is not unknown. But it usually lasts one night only, like the flu for a day."

"We call it the twenty-four hour flu. Anyway, the restaurant functioned fine without him on the second day. You can easily do his job."

"It is one thing for the *chef de cuisine* to disappear. It is quite another when the customers disappear as well."

"But Tuesday was crowded even after the bad reviews."

"Yes, and Wednesday less so. Thursday was even worse, and each day the number of covers grows smaller. This week was terrible. Last night we had only four."

"For the whole night? On a Saturday?"

He nodded.

"I don't think Kuchen coming back can help."

"Ah, precisely so. I am glad you understand this. It is not the chef that must change. It is the menu."

"So this meeting is about changing the menu?"

"*Non!* This meeting is about closing the restaurant."

His angular head was canted to the side in an unnatural way, causing him to look like one of the figures in Picasso's *Les Demoiselles d'Avignon*. "You must help. It will not be easy, but you are the one. You must help us."

"You want me to help close the restaurant?"

"*Sacré bleu, non*. You must help us keep it open."

Before I could figure out how to respond to that strange request, M'Lanta Scruggs called us into the dining room. We were the last two to be seated. All of the staff were there except Kuchen. Even the assistants from the kitchen and scullery were there. Scruggs, whose duties evidently included delivering messages and gathering people together, went to the kitchen and returned with Santiago Molinero.

The sight of his copper-tinged skin brought *Moulin Rouge* to mind, although I know that *rouge* means red, not copper. Maybe he looked like one of the bar flies in a Toulouse-Lautrec poster. Or perhaps his face was flushed because he was facing an unpleasant task.

"I suspect most of you have figured out why I called this meeting," he began. Juan the bacon chopper whispered a translation for his *compadres* who didn't speak English.

Santiago looked around the room. "*Schnitzel* has failed." There were no gasps. He looked around again. He rubbed his beard. He seemed to reconsider his words. "Actually, it is I who have failed. I saw Santa Fe as a great restaurant town, which it is. I asked myself how a new restaurant could succeed against all the competition, and I thought the answer was to bring a cuisine not represented here. I sold that idea to the investors. They knew a restaurant that succeeds in Santa Fe would make money. They agreed that a new cuisine was the best plan. Obviously, Austrian cuisine was a poor choice. So too was my choice of Gunter Kuchen who deserted us after opening night. But I cannot blame him. I can blame only myself. You have all worked hard and done your best. I apologize."

"So what happens now?" asked Helen Mure.

"I will file bankruptcy papers. In cases such as this, the stockholders will get nothing. It is the risk of investment. The judge will declare their stock worthless. You will be treated better than they. An auction company will sell off the equipment. The money will go into an escrow account to pay your salaries and our creditors."

"How long will it take?"

"Probably six month or so."

Alain stood up and looked around the room, his angular chin pointing to each of us in turn. "I have rallied the staff. We agree that *Schnitzel* has failed. But we are not *Schnitzel*. We are a *compagnie*. Say what you must about Kuchen, but he welded us together in the forge of his temper. We will resurrect this restaurant under a new banner. The public will know we have thrown off the shackles of tradition and embraced innovation. We will turn the Austrian eagle into a phoenix in the desert. We will rise from the ashes!"

I thought I heard strains of *La Marseillaise* in the background.

"*Bravo*," bellowed Dorfmeister.

"*Allez*," cried Machlin Masoot.

"*C'est magnifique*," shouted Raoul Deschutes.

"What a load of bullshit," barked Helen Mure.

Everyone glared at her.

"What do you have in mind specifically?" asked Molinero, uncertainty washing over his face.

"We will be the first Austrian/Southwestern fusion restaurant in history," he proclaimed proudly. "We cannot abandon totally the beginnings. We have the training and the supplies. Also, we are known. Perhaps badly, but even that is a start. As we say in France, the woman without a questionable past has no chance to reform."

We all turned to him with quizzical looks.

"Perhaps it does not translate well into English. But the diners will want to know what is this upstart that fell so badly on the nose and now dares to reinvent itself with the local flavors."

"It is an interesting proposal," said Molinero, "but we are in no position to carry it out. We are out of money. We cannot continue."

"Sure we can," said Rafael. "It doesn't cost anything to keep the doors open. Even if we can't pay the rent, it will take at least a couple of months for the landlord to have us evicted. The utility companies don't shut off service until you're behind several months. By then, we may be making money. And we already have enough food to last us for a couple for weeks."

Mure said, "So you want to stiff the landlord and the utility companies and operate like squatters in the building?"

"They're going to get stiffed anyway if we close. I want to stay open and try to earn enough money to pay them."

"But there is no money to pay you," said Molinero.

"So what is different about this?" replied Alain. "We have food. We will not starve."

"What I get paid," said Scruggs, "it's no big loss not to get it."

"Not getting paid is the story of my life," said Arliss Mansfield.

"I refuse to work for free," Mure hissed.

"We want only those who believe in our plan," said Alain.

Maria Salazar said, "I believe in it. If Helen leaves, I'll volunteer to take her station."

"Forget it, you little tart. Nobody's taking my station."

Maria stared at her but made no comment.

"It just isn't possible," said Molinero.

"And how do you propose to stop us?" asked Jürgen.

Molinero took a step back as if Jürgen's question were a blow. "I beg your pardon?"

"We have keys to the building. We know our equipment. We have a plan. We will have a grand re-opening on Wednesday night."

"This is preposterous," shouted Molinero.

"It is rather odd," Arliss noted, more or less to himself.

"I say close up and go home," said Mure.

"No!" shouted most of the others.

Molinero seemed to regain his composure. "What is your plan?" Alain said, "For simplicity, we will invent six new dishes, three starters and three entrées, all in the new style of Austrian/Southwestern fusion. Our menu will be *prix fixe*, nineteen dollars."

"Nineteen dollars? You will lose money."

Jürgen laughed. "We have no money to lose."

"And how will you invent these dishes? You are Frenchmen and Austrians. Even the Americans among you have never worked in a Southwestern restaurant. Not a single one of you knows anything about Southwestern ingredients and flavors."

"That is where you are mistaken," said Alain. "We have on our staff an expert *première classe* in the Southwestern cuisine."

He looked my way. I turned to see who the expert behind me might be. Then I heard him say my name.

Molinero scoffed. "He's a ceramic artist, not a cook."

"Ah," said Alain, "that is where you are once again wrong. In his conversations with us, he has revealed himself to have the experience and, most importantly, the palate."

Maria Salazar added, "When Hubie and I lunched at *La Casa Sena*, he understood the menu better than I did and explained about the different varieties of *chiles*."

"Yeah," said Mure, "and I can just imagine what the dessert was."

"You're just jealous that I like men rather than women."

"You're a restaurant slut."

"And you're a dyke."

"Ladies, ladies!" shouted Dorfmeister. The two of them sunk into their chairs and glared at each other.

Masoot said to Molinero, "You did not taste the dish he prepared for the staff on the day of the opening." He brought his pursed fingers to his lips and blew them open in tribute to my *mole*.

Santiago looked like the superintendent of a mental hospital whose patients have announced they are taking over the institution. No one said anything for a full minute. Finally, Molinero asked, "All those in favor of this new plan, raise your hands."

Before we could vote, Juan said, "Pardon me, Mr. Molinero. I have been translating for those who do not speak English. But because this is an important vote, I feel it would be proper for you to say it to them rather than me."

Molinero frowned and hesitated. Then he shrugged and said, "*Si les gusta este nuevo plan, levanten los manos.*"

I winced when he said it. His Spanish was even worse than Dolly's.

Every hand went up except for Wallace Voile, who had remained impassive and silent throughout the meeting.

Alain stood up again and said triumphantly, "So we are together. *Fraternité!*"

Molinero said, "I wish you luck," and retreated to his office.

Alain announced we would reconvene in an hour to begin planning the new dishes. Jürgen went outside to smoke. Maria headed for the women's room. Several guys headed to the men's room. Wallace went out the front door. The rest went into the kitchen.

I sat in my chair dumfounded.

Alain came and sat next to me. "What did you think of my speech?"

"A little over the top."

"Then it is perhaps well that I cut the last line."

"Which was?"

"*Succès ou la Mort!*"

I stared at him and he laughed. "Can you not tell when I make the joke? I practice the speech in front of a mirror. I was not trying to convince the staff. They had agreed before the meeting."

"You thought the speech would convince Molinero?"

"No, I thought it would, as you say, throw him off his walk."

"Throw him off his stride," I corrected.

"Precisely."

39

My natural inclination was to find a corner and hide in it while trying to figure out what had just happened.

Plan B would have been to tell Alain he had the wrong guy. I'm not good under pressure or working with groups. Then again, that seemed to be a common trait of the people at *Schnitzel*.

So I decided to roll with the plan. I drove to the produce market—actual slogan: "A fast nickel beats a slow dime"—and bought jalapeños, poblanos, *habañeros* and cucumbers.

Alain gathered the staff at one of the work stations when I returned and asked me for the first dish. I looked at him, Helen Mure, Jürgen Dorfmeister, Machlin Masoot, Maria Salazar, Raoul Deschutes, Arliss Mansfield and Rafael Pacheco. I felt like an altar boy preparing to instruct the Pope on theology.

"What is a *schnitzel*," I asked Jürgen.

"It is simply meat with a crust."

"And a *weinerschnitzel*?"

"'*Wein*' is the Austrian name for Vienna. They like veal, so a *weinerschnitzel* is a veal cutlet with a crust."

"Can you use pork?"

"Of course, but it is then called *wienerschnitzel vom schwein*."

"And suppose it was made in New Mexico. What would you call it then?"

"A bad joke," snarled Mure.

"A *chile schnitzel*," said Maria.

"*Voilà!*" cried Alain. "This will be our new name."

"Oh, brother," said Mure.

"I don't know," added Arliss.

Masoot said, "I like it. I have toyed with the idea of a *chile* dessert."

"Now I've heard it all," said Mure.

"We'll get to the dessert later," I said. I swallowed hard. "I want to show you how to prepare our new signature dish—*schnitzel con tres chiles*."

I stepped up to a stainless steel work surface and emptied the bag of produce.

"I will be your *assistante*," said Alain as he stepped beside me.

"Me too," said Rafael, stepping to my other side.

I had no idea where everything was. "I need a knife."

Alain asked, "A chef's knife, a carving knife, a paring knife, a serrated knife, a boning knife, a filleting knife, a—"

"Stop!"

This was insane. I turned to look at the group. "I have no idea what I'm doing here. I like to cook, but cooking at home and cooking professionally are worlds apart. I have only two knives in my kitchen. I appreciate what you're trying to do, but your confidence in me to help you do it is misplaced. I am not a chef."

"Don't worry," said Alain. "We will do the cooking. We look to you for the ideas." He smiled at me. "What do you call your two knives?"

"The big one and the little one," I said and heard Maria giggle.

"Do you want a big knife or a little one?" asked Alain.

"A little one, please."

I used it to slice the stem end off a dozen large jalapeños. The thing being sharp as a razor made the task easy, but it was scary to wield. I sliced the jalapeños lengthwise and removed the ribs and seeds. I pushed the prepared jalapeños aside and picked up a cucumber.

"Do you want them peeled?" asked Rafael.

I said I did, and he made short work of them.

"Seeds?" he asked.

"Out. And I need them sliced."

He halved the cukes longwise and removed the seeds deftly with a spoon. He sliced them so quickly and uniformly that no machine could have been more precise. He then ran a hand over them, arraying them like the cards of a deck. It was a shame to see the slices so perfectly displayed because they were destined for the blender.

I moved to a cooktop and cranked the flame to its highest position. I selected a deep pot to avoid splattering and coated the bottom liberally with corn oil. When the oil was just starting to smoke, I threw in the jalapeños and stirred them vigorously. After about a minute, I yelled, "sugar" because I had forgotten to have it at hand. Arliss grabbed a plastic container from an overhead rack and thrust it in front of me. I took half a handful and dumped it in the pot. I hope this won't shock you, but I had been watching them cook for weeks, and I knew they used their hands freely.

I gave the jalapeños one last stir to coat them with the sugar. Some of the skins had begun to darken, but they had not burned, which was exactly what I wanted. I pulled the pot off the heat and covered it.

We returned to the work surface. Maria brought me a blender.

"The *saucier* should do this," I said.

She smiled. "Maybe later. For now, I prefer to watch and learn."

The blender looked like something you might see in an auto repair shop, maybe something used to grind down pistons. I don't know what pistons do or whether they have to be ground down, but that's what came to mind.

I threw in the jalapeños, the cucumbers and some heavy cream. I looked around for a button or switch but couldn't find one. Maria placed the lid on the device. When she twisted it, the beast roared to life. From the noise the device made, I didn't know whether the ingredients were being blended or vaporized. She shut it off quickly. I spooned out a bit and tasted it. The texture was perfect. I added a bit of salt and pepper. I tasted again. It was the taste I hoped for. But what would the professionals think?

Just in case you are wondering, I used a second spoon for the second taste. But then I'm more fastidious than the average cook.

Maria tasted it and said, "Splendid."

"Gimme that spoon," said Mure. She took a taste. After a worrying hesitation, she turned to me. "It *is* good," she said, her voice showing genuine surprise.

Alain was next. "*Délicieux*. But I am surprised it is not hotter. I am also surprised you used no stock for the sauce."

"Caramelizing the jalapeños leaves them hot but without the sting. Cucumbers are mostly liquid, and they're lighter than chicken stock. They give a fresh taste without changing the flavor."

"Amazing," said Maria.

Everyone praised the sauce, although I thought some of their enthusiasm arose from the general optimism they had adopted as a necessary attitude for embarking on the quixotic mission to resurrect *Schnitzel*.

"It is as delicious as everyone says," said Jürgen, "but do you propose to use this on a *schnitzel*?"

"Yes. It is the first of the three chiles in *schnitzel con tres chiles*. The second one will be a *habañero* relish. The jalapeño sauce can be ladled directly on the *schnitzel* because it is mild by New Mexico standards, but the *habañero* relish will be fiery and will need to be on the side."

I showed them how to make it by boiling finely chopped *habañeros*, purple onions and chopped cilantro in sugar and vinegar.

The third chile was in the starch that would be paired with the *schnitzel*—roasted, peeled and chopped poblanos added to creamy *spätzle*. Jürgen tried to defend the integrity of Austrian cuisine by drawing a line at poblano *spätzle*, but after it had been prepared and tasted, he relented.

Alain suggested the staff prepare enough of the new dish for our evening meal and shooed me out of the kitchen. I sat in the dining room expecting at any minute that the person who drew the short straw would come through the swinging door to tell me that although they appreciated my effort, my assistance would no longer be needed.

But when the door finally opened, they emerged carrying plates of *schnitzel con tres chiles*, Scruggs with two plates so that I had one as well. Alain suggested we open several bottles of *Grüner Veltliner*, which he thought would pair well with the dish, but Arliss reminded him we had no funds to replenish our supplies and argued that the wine should be saved for paying customers. Alain agreed, although it saddened me to see a Frenchman eating dinner without wine. I remembered him sharing his *croque monsieur* with me and wished I could do the same for him with a bottle of Austria's national wine. Or, even better, a bottle of Gruet, which no one will be surprised to hear I thought would be a better pairing. I decided to do something about the fact that *Schnitzel* did not stock America's best champagne.

Although it was only six when we finished eating, we were emotionally spent. We decided to tackle the next dish in the morning. Before heading home, I went to the grocery store on St. Francis and bought some Gruet. I returned to the restaurant, but didn't go in because I saw Arliss Mansfield leaving. The building was dark.

After he was safely away, I went inside and put the Gruet in the bar refrigerator. And wondered why first Scruggs and now Mansfield had reason to visit the restaurant late at night when no one else was around.

40

"*Chile schnitzel?* You can't be serious?"

It was later that same evening, and Susannah was sitting at my kitchen table finishing up the *schnitzel con tres chiles* I brought from Santa Fe and warmed in my oven.

"This dish is great," she said, "but you can't name a restaurant after it."

"If we named the restaurant after it, we'd have to call it *schnitzel con tres chiles*. You like that better?"

"I don't like either one. You can't put '*chile*' and '*schnitzel*' together. Who ever heard of *schnitzel* in New Mexico?"

"No one ever heard of a hurricane in New Mexico, either, but we have *Hurricane's Drive In* right here in Albuquerque."

"Yeah, and we also have *Cake Fetish Cupcakes* and *Lumpy's Burgers*, so what does that prove?"

Nothing, so far as I could tell.

I grabbed a piece of paper and my box of colored pencils and wrote *Chile Schnitzel* with *chile* in what looked to me like a Southwestern font, simple and informal, and *schnitzel* in what I took to be an Austrian-looking style. I made the word *chile* green for the famous New Mexico green chiles and the word *schnitzel* red for the Austrian flag.

She said, "It looks pretty, but it still doesn't go together."

"That's the whole point. Fusion. Two very different things. Two fonts, two colors, two cuisines. And the colors are red and green."

She rolled her eyes. "I know, New Mexico's official state question—Red or Green? Don't you think it's a little embarrassing that other states have state birds and state songs, and we have a state question?"

"It must have been a slow day in the legislature."

"So what's next?"

"I need to come up with five more dishes, three starters and two more entrées. You work in a restaurant, help me out here."

"I'm a server, not a cook."

"What do most people order?"

"Enchiladas. Maybe you could have enchiladas filled with *schnitzel*."

It was an indication of my desperation that I briefly considered it. When I regained my senses, I said, "Jürgen mentioned his favorite dish growing up was *Wurstknoedel*, stuffed potato dumplings. That's sort of like an enchilada, except with potato on the outside rather than tortillas."

"What would you put inside?"

"I don't know. What does *La Placita* put in their enchiladas?"

"The usual—beef, cheese or chicken. We even have a vegetarian one with mushrooms and *calabacitas*. But my favorites are the ones with chicken *mole*."

And that's how I came up with the second entrée.

41

Inspired by my conversation with Susannah and having my pencils at hand, I started sketching *chiles* and *ristras* after she left.

I set them against a round background and played with different ways to position them, going so far at one point as to create a sort of *chile* version of the *Vitruvian Man* by Leonardo da Vinci. It looked silly. Also not quite so well drawn as Leonardo's.

I finally settled on two *chiles*—one red and one green, of course—tied together at their stems, their tips protruding slightly over the edge of the plate at different lengths. I didn't want symmetry, fearful or otherwise.

I dropped the drawing off at Feats of Clay on my way to Santa Fe the next morning along with instructions about what I wanted. They agreed to make the switch at no extra charge since they had not yet created and applied the edelweiss overlays.

I arrived at *Schnitzel* to find I was not the only one whose creative juices had been flowing. Rafael had come up with all three new appetizers—grilled duck breast with a sauce made from dried New Mexico cherries, smoked New Mexico trout with a piñon and apricot pesto and a Caesar salad with *Verdolagas* instead of romaine and an egg yolk dressing infused with garlic and cumin. *Verdolaga* is a Mexican green, a sort of cross between watercress and frisee.

I asked Rafael if he had stayed up all night.

"It was easy. I just remembered what Dagmar Mortensen had written about my salads. Fear is a great motivator."

"Susannah was worried about you when I told her about the reviews. I have to say I was shocked when I read what Dagmar wrote."

He shrugged. "She was right. Those salads were awful. And you can tell Susannah not to worry. I don't feel bad because it wasn't my fault. Nobody could make a bologna salad taste good. I could have improved the potato salad, but Kuchen insisted I stick to the recipe."

"I wonder where he is."

"Back in Austria would be my guess."

I found Masoot experimenting with ways to incorporate Southwestern flavors into the crusty *boules* served at *Schnitzel*. I told him about my idea for a *crème brûlée* with *chipotle* sugar, and he asked me to produce some of the flavored sugar for him. That sent me to the grocery store for a can of *chipotles* which I drained and put in the food drier.

I passed along the idea of a *Wurstknoedel* filled with chicken *mole* to Alain and gave him my recipe for *mole*. He grabbed the recipe like a kid reaching for a new toy and walked away reading it. After about six steps, he came back. "It is complicated, no? Perhaps we can prepare the first batch together."

As we went through the steps, Alain changed some of the processes to make them faster and easier. Kitchen skills seem so simple, but watching a pro slice and dice made me feel like a klutz.

When all the ingredients were in the giant pot for the *mole*, I sought out Jürgen and found him experimenting with different spices in the breading for the pork cutlets that would become the *schnitzel*. I hadn't thought of that. He was busy and enjoying himself, so I left him alone and went to check the food drier, only to find Masoot had unloaded it and was grinding the dried *chipotles* with sugar in a mortar and pestle.

Juan was de-stemming and de-seeding jalapeños. Deschutes was filleting trout in preparation for smoking. Maria was making piñon and apricot pesto. Helen Mure was working with potatoes. Rafael had left to search for a source of *Verdolagas*.

Everyone except me had a task to perform and was busily and enthusiastically performing it. I had invented *schnitzel con tres chiles*, but I wouldn't be the one cooking it. Susannah had given me the idea of stuffing *mole* into a potato dumpling which, when you think about it, hardly rates up there with inventing the wheel. Rafael, by comparison, had come up with three outstanding ideas and had the wherewithal to implement them. Masoot was off and running with the new *chipotle* sugar *crème brûlée*. Alain was making *mole* faster than I could and no doubt better.

Even Scruggs ran me out of the scullery when I went to talk with him. "You got everybody cooking out there, Shoes. That's good. Gives a lot of work for me and the boys."

I started to reply, but he yelled, "Step aside," and I moved just in time to avoid being run over by a kid with a pile of greasy pans.

I went to the bar and sat on a stool. Kaiser Wilhelm II was so impressed with Escoffier's cooking that he said to him, "I am the Emperor of Germany, but you are the emperor of chefs." I was not the emperor of food. I wasn't even a general of gastronomy. More like a peasant of provisions.

No one missed me. My brief flirtation with professional chef-dom had come to an end. I wondered what I would do if by some miracle the plan succeeded. What if *Chile Schnitzel* became a money-making restaurant? What would my role be? I was no professional cook. I had no clue about waiting tables. I lack the personality to be a bartender. I'd probably be a poor potscrubber, and I didn't think Scruggs would want me anyway.

Maybe I could be a greeter like they have at Wal-Mart, I thought to myself in comic relief.

Then it came to me. In addition to being a treasure hunter—aka pot thief—I was also a merchant. I had a business degree and had worked briefly as an accountant. I could be the money manager.

If we made any. If we gave the money to Molinero, he would probably just waste it on things like rent and back expenses. What we *should* do with it was purchase supplies and pay the staff. They were enthusiastic about Alain's plan, but you can't eat enthusiasm. Eventually, they would have to be paid.

But how? Most diners pay with a credit card, and our machine would funnel the money into an account controlled by Molinero. It sounded like a job for Tristan.

Scruggs called dinner at five. It was like a smorgasbord because we had samples of all the new dishes. No one had come up with the third new entrée, but we had more than just the three appetizers and the two entrées because various renditions had been prepared for comparison. Maria had drawn up a scoring sheet and someone had stuck numbered sticky notes on the dishes.

There was an air of excitement as everyone tasted and commented. Even Helen Mure put aside her attitude, and no one was upset when someone suggested a change to another person's dish.

As we were finishing up the *crème brûlées*, Alain stood up and read us the text of an advertisement he had placed in the newspaper.

"This is to announce that the restaurant formerly known as *Schnitzel* has been attacked by an alien *chile* from Roswell. It is holding the staff hostage and forcing us to add Southwestern flavors to our dishes. Please join us for our Grand Re-opening on Thursday night as *Chile Schnitzel*, the world's first Austrian/Southwestern fusion restaurant."

Jaws dropped. People glanced at each other. After a few seconds of silence, Jürgen roared with laughter. "He is joking."

"But of course," said Alain, "the Grand Re-opening is Wednesday, not Thursday."

42

I walked to *La Fonda* and entered the bar.

Curiosity about all the new dishes had caused me to overeat. I needed a *digestif.*

The problem was I had no idea what one is. It sounds like a drink to settle your tummy. Maybe it's a brand-name, I thought.

But when I asked the bartender for a *digestif,* he asked which one.

"Surprise me," I said, and he brought me a small glass of Campari. It tasted like something that would *cause* digestive problems, not ameliorate them.

"Something not so bitter," I told the barman when he noticed I had stopped drinking the Campari. He brought me a Fernet-Branca. I have no idea what it was made from, but it was peppery and sweet. Better than the Campari, but not something you could sip all evening.

The next one was grappa. It was not something I ever plan to drink again, but it cleared my sinuses and encouraged me to try again. Francisco—we were on a first name basis at this point—suggested Lillet. It was lighter than the others with a pleasant citrus tang, but it was basically wine. I don't like wine unless it has bubbles.

Next came pastis. If it had been the first drink of the evening, I would have hated it. I don't like licorice. But after the others, it was strangely smoothing. I actually drank the entire glass.

I should have stopped there. Actually, I should have stopped at the bar door and never entered. But my buddy Francisco insisted I try Cynar. By this time, distilled pickle juice would have tasted like the nectar of the gods. Cynar, on the other hand, tasted like tarnished pennies. It wasn't so much a taste as a sensation, a fibrillation of the muscles in the throat.

I shook my head and blinked my eyes. I rolled my head around my shoulders like someone with a stiff neck.

Then I took another taste and identified the flavor. Artichokes.

"I'll have another," I said.

I went to my room, but the key wouldn't open the door. Then I remembered Molinero saying I could have the room through the Grand Opening, so I went to the desk and charged the room on my credit card. I was in no shape to drive back to Albuquerque, and I was not going to sleep in the Bronco and risk ending up dead as another person.

Strange thoughts run through your brain after six *digestifs*.

I awoke the next morning around nine with a fiery stomach and a pounding head.

I bought a bottle of Mylanta Extra Strength in the gift shop, chugged some down and went directly to the French Café where I drank three cups of strong coffee to kill the taste of the Mylanta and soothe my headache. When I reached into my pocket for a tip, I came out with my bar bill from last night. Seventy-three dollars.

Which was small change compared to my room bill. When I went to the front desk to drop my key, the clerk gave me an invoice for $3,986.72.

"There must be some mistake," I said, pushing the paper back to him.

He studied it for a moment. "No, sir. It is correct. Twenty-one nights plus tax and bar charges."

I have to cut back on my drinking, I thought to myself—those bar charges really mount up. Then I realized he had said twenty-one nights.

"But I charged only last night. All the previous nights were charged to *Schnitzel*, the restaurant I'm working for."

He stared at his computer screen. "Yes, the record says billed to a third party, but the bill has not been paid, so when you presented a credit card, the entire amount was automatically charged to your card."

"But I only intended to pay for a single night."

"Perhaps you can get your employer to reimburse you."

Fat chance. I argued with the clerk briefly. He was a friendly and able chap but unauthorized to reverse charges. He gave me the manager's card and suggested I contact him when he returned to work the next day.

I drank the rest of the Mylanta.

43

I stopped by *Schnitzel* and saw Alain on a ladder over the front door painting the word '*chile*' next to the word '*schnitzel*' above the lintel. My font suggestion had been ignored.

The Austrian flag to the right of the door remained, but the one on the left had been replaced by its red and yellow New Mexican counterpart.

After ascertaining I was even more useless to them than I had been the day before, I drove to Albuquerque, stopping at Gruet for more champagne in order to have enough to serve for the Grand Re-Opening.

But which I didn't come away with because my credit card was rejected as being over the limit. Gina the manager was friendly, competent and apologetic, but of course it was the bank's fault, and there was nothing she could do. Actually, it wasn't the bank's fault. It was *Schnitzels*' fault. Then, after reflecting on it and facing the ugly truth, I realized it was my own fault. Everyone had warned me about restaurants, Susannah even urging me to get paid in advance.

The next hour was spent on credit card matters. First I called Tristan. He said he could probably reprogram our credit card machine. Then I called my own credit card company. After almost an hour and a dozen attempts at navigating their phone menu and pushing buttons, I got a guy with a thick Bengali accent who agreed to note on the record that I was contesting the charge from *La Fonda*. That didn't make me feel any better, in part because I figured nothing would come of it, but also because *La Fonda* deserved to be paid. I just didn't want to be the one doing the paying. I was in a foul mood at that point, so I took Geronimo for a long walk. His company and the burned energy perked me up.

But my mood deteriorated when I found Whit Fletcher at my door at the end of my walk.

He didn't even let me unlock the door before he waved a paper in my face. "This here's a warrant for your arrest for the murder of Barry Stiles."

Suddenly my four thousand dollar hotel bill seemed like a minor issue.

"I was afraid of this. Duran wants to force me to finger Dorfmeister, and since I won't do that, he makes me the suspect."

"You got a pretty low opinion of Duran to say a thing like that."

"Why else would he accuse me? I have no motive for killing Barry. I hardly even knew the guy."

"I guess they'll try to figure out the motive later. Duran tells me this here warrant was issued on the basis of means and opportunity."

"Opportunity? Stiles being found in my vehicle isn't opportunity. The window was open. Everyone in Santa Fe had as much opportunity as I did. As to means, how does that relate to me? I don't even know how he was killed."

Maybe you have an inkling of the means if you've been paying attention, but I didn't until Whit looked down at his little notebook and asked, "You know anything about a chemical called barium carbonate?"

I knew a lot about it as an ingredient in glazes. And I immediately figured out something else I knew about it; namely, that the container of it I used in Santa Fe did not have a leak or a loose-fitting lid as I had surmised when I saw the level was lower than I remembered. It was lower because someone had used some of it to poison Barry Stiles.

"Well?" Whit prompted.

"It's a chemical used in pottery glazes."

"I guess that would give you the means, you being a pottery guy."

"I still say Duran is trying to pressure me. Barry died three weeks ago. If Duran thought the barium carbonate made me a suspect, why did he wait so long to get a warrant?"

"He just found out about it. They found a fresh needle mark when they did the autopsy on Stiles and a bump on his head that the coroner said was from a blow that was probably strong enough to knock him out but not enough to kill him. So they figured someone conked him on the noggin and shot him full of poison. Trouble is, the toxicology scan didn't show any poison. There was evidence of a heart attack, so the coroner was thinking about going with that old standby, natural causes. Then Duran got an anonymous phone call on Sunday telling him Stiles died from barium carbonate poisoning. Seems barium carbonate is not one of the chemicals the toxicology scan tests for. That was pretty sharp of you, Hubert, to use a poison they wouldn't find. If your accomplice hadn't ratted you out, you would've gotten away with it."

"Accomplice? I didn't have an accomplice."

"You done it all by yourself?"

"I didn't do it at all, by myself or with an accomplice."

"Think about it Hubert. Like you say, you got no reason to kill Stiles. Dorkmaster and Stiles had some sort of a run-in at the restaurant, maybe argued about whose silly hat should be taller. So Dorkmaster—"

"Dorfmeister."

"Whatever. He decides to get you to help him. I can't see you sticking a needle in anybody, so he probably just asked you to supply the poison, knowing you would get blamed."

"But I didn't get blamed. Nobody did. Since the coroner ruled natural causes, why would Jürgen implicate me by tipping Duran about the barium carbonate?"

"The coroner hasn't filed his ruling yet, so your friend was still waiting for the shoe to drop. He got tired of waiting and decided to speed things along by calling Duran. But the good news is that if you tell Duran what really happened, you can probably get off with just accessory before the fact." Then he apparently had a brainstorm. "Matter of fact, you could just say he borrowed some of that barium stuff, and you had no idea what he wanted it for. You might walk on this one."

"I've got a better story. The barium carbonate was stolen from me, and I had nothing to do with the murder. And the best part about that story is it's true."

He looked disappointed. "Now when did truth ever have anything to do with it? What matters is what a jury believes. You try your story and you come off as a guy trying to wash his hands of any responsibility. But you say you were duped by a friend, and you get the sympathy vote."

I told him I preferred to stick to the truth, and he told me I could call someone to look after Geronimo before going to the police station.

44

I called Layton Kent.

He would be a poor choice as a dog-sitter.

He would worry about getting dog hair on his suit. He is, however, the perfect man to call if you need a get-out-of-jail card. He showed up at the police station in a dark blue wool suit tailored to fit his three-hundred pound body perfectly. There was a silk handkerchief in his breast pocket and a Patek Philippe Sky Moon Tourbillon watch on his wrist which probably cost him more than the gross national product of Nicaragua. His hair was slicked back without a part, his face unblemished, his fingernails freshly manicured. He always has an air of royalty about him, although it is his wife, Mariella, who is said to be descended from Don Francisco Fernandez de la Cueva Enriquez, *Duque de Alburquerque*, the man after whom our fair city is named, minus a now famously missing first 'r'.

Layton is the most prominent attorney in town and Mariella the most prominent socialite. His law practice is devoted almost exclusively to crafting documents that allow one to avoid taxes, and his clients are the people most in need of such services. That would be the fabulously wealthy. The rest of us would not benefit from his services because the fees he charges exceed the taxes we pay.

He stoops to practice criminal law only when a current client needs it, and—undeservedly—I am one of those clients. Indeed, I have required his assistance in so many criminal cases that he would have dropped me long ago were it not for the fact that Mariella is a collector of traditional Native American pots from New Mexico's pueblos, and I am her personal dealer.

We were shown to an interrogation room and left alone, a treatment those represented by a public defender probably do not receive.

"Well, Hubert. It has been almost six months since you were charged with a murder. Since none of my other clients have run afoul of the law in the interim, I was beginning to fear my criminal defense skills would atrophy. I suppose I should thank you for giving me an opportunity to stay at the top of my game."

The pompous jackass part comes with the great attorney part, so I just ignored it and told him the entire story, during which time he had his eyes closed and his fingertips formed in a temple and resting gently against his lips. He insists on every detail no matter how small or seemingly unimportant, so it took me almost an hour to tell it all.

He remained still after I ceased my narrative. Had I not known him so well, I would have thought him asleep.

"Barry Stiles worked at Café Alsace," he finally said, making me wonder why he noted that particular fact. "I ate there when it first opened. The food was unpalatable."

Layton fancies himself a gourmet.

"Arliss Mansfield, Rafael Pacheco and Wallace Voile also worked there," he said. "Are you certain no others at *Schnitzel* were previously at Alsace?"

"Yes. Since Rafael is now at *Schnitzel*, I'm sure he would have recognized any former Alsace employees. He said just those three."

"And the food was also bad at *Schnitzel*."

"It will be much better when they re-open tomorrow," I said.

He waved a hand dismissively. "Stiles' death is likely rooted in something that happened at Alsace. But that is a matter to explore at trial in order to argue that other potential perpetrators are more plausible than you. Those would be Arliss Mansfield, Rafael Pacheco and Wallace Voile. Means never trumps motive. And I would wager one of them has a motive. Furthermore, everyone working at *Schnitzel* had as much access to the barium carbonate as you did since your work area had no door and you were frequently not in it."

His reasoning was sound but one of his premises was flawed, although I didn't realize it at the time.

"I'm surprised Duran was able to get a warrant," he noted.

"But he did, and now I'm in jail."

He finally opened his eyes. "Don't be melodramatic, Hubert. You are not in jail. You are merely at the police station, and you will not be here much longer. I called Judge Aragon before coming down here."

And right on cue, one of his beautiful young paralegals came in with a signed motion to quash the warrant.

45

I had forgotten we still lacked a third Austrian/Southwestern entrée.

Being arrested for murder will do that.

So when Layton dropped me off in Old Town, I walked over to Miss Gladys' Gift Shop and found her sitting behind her counter crocheting something.

Or maybe she was knitting. She was doing the one that requires a hook, whichever that is. She usually brings me her casseroles, so she was pleased I actually came seeking a recipe.

I explained that we needed something like *tafelspitz*, beef tips cooked in broth and usually served with sour cream and potatoes.

Her eyes lit up. "Oh, that would be Melba Mason's Tender Tips Supreme. Her husband was pastor of the Holiness Temple. She served her Tender Tips every summer at the revival and never even knew all the men were washing it down with whiskey they kept hidden in the porta-potties behind the tent. She just figured they were going out back so often because of her sweet tea."

She listed the ingredients as sirloin tips coated in flour and browned, chopped green onions, frozen hash browns, canned mushroom soup, canned beef broth, Worcestershire sauce, ketchup and the ingredient that told me we had to try this—ginger ale.

After convincing her I didn't want her to cook some for me, I went directly to *Dos Hermanas* and told Susannah she had been right.

"About what?" she asked, looking at me over the saltless rim of her otherwise perfect margarita.

"About everything. You said I would become a suspect, and today I was arrested. You said Barry Stiles was injected with poison, and he was." I shook my head in amazement. "I'm surprised you didn't also figure out the poison was one of my glazing chemicals."

"I didn't know glazing chemicals are poison."

"Neither did I. There's a fume hood in my workshop, but they have those in the restaurant, too. I figured the city required me to have it merely because any fumes are bad for your lungs. I never guessed I was working with poison."

"What poison is it?"

"Barium carbonate."

"Oh, rat poison."

"What? You've heard of it?"

"Yeah, we use it on the ranch."

"Okay, you seem to know everything about this whole situation, so who killed Barry Stiles?"

"Wallace Voile."

"Really?" I felt like I had just stepped through the looking glass. "Why?"

"First, there's her name."

"You said it was romantic." *Maybe Rafael thinks so, too*, I thought to myself.

"It's romantic when the last name is Simpson. But no one names girls Wallace, so Voile is using an alias, and people who do that usually have something to hide."

"That seems a little weak."

"You haven't heard it all. Second, she worked at Café Alsace, so she has a previous connection with Barry."

"So do Arliss and Rafael."

"Why do you always call him Rafael?"

I turned up a palm. "I like the name, I guess."

"Anyway, from the way you described Arliss, I can't see him as a murderer, and I *know* Ice didn't do it."

I ate some salsa on a chip and washed it down with a margarita properly attired with a salty rim. Then I just sat there.

"Okay," she said, "I didn't think hmm zuu was a murderer either, and I was wrong. But this time I'm not."

"Hmm zuu?"

"I promised myself not to mention his name any more."

"Oh, him." I hoped she was right. "What else?" I asked.

"In addition to using an alias and having a past connection with the victim, Voile is the perfect villain because she is so unlikely. The beautiful woman who seems to have it all. She doesn't kill men— they kill for her."

"That may be the way it works in fiction, but in real life the murderer is usually the most obvious suspect. Although I admit I could see her sneaking up behind Barry, clocking him with a hammer then jabbing a needle full of poison into him. She seems cold-blooded enough to do that. But why?"

"Jeez," she said jokingly, "I already figured out who did it. The least you could do is supply the motive."

46

"Our second grand Opening in a month," I said to Jürgen and Alain.

Jürgen contradicted me. "It is not the second because it is a *re-opening.*"

Alain wagged a finger. "*Non.* It is a Grand Opening. We are no longer *Schnitzel.* We are *Chile Schnitzel.*"

"Doesn't roll trippingly off the tongue, does it?" said Jürgen.

Alain shrugged. "We will see what the public thinks."

I handed them each a copy of what I had labeled *Tafelspitz Sangre de Cristo.* The green onions had been replaced with *chiles*, the hash browns with fresh potatoes, and the ketchup had given way to enchilada sauce. The dish was topped with crema Mexicana mixed with horseradish.

Alain looked up from the paper. "What is ginger ale?"

"The key ingredient," I said.

He took a sip from a cold can I had brought with me. "Ah. It is like the strange ginger beer the English drink, but the American one is weaker." He shuddered. "And sweeter."

"Ginger beer would work better with the beef," said Jürgen.

"The recipe is yours," I said to them. "Do with it as you please."

"I will go to buy Ginger Beer and *tafelspitz*," said Jürgen.

I was confused. "I thought we would *make* the *tafelspitz*, not buy it."

"*Tafelspitz* is a cut of meat from the tritip."

"If you can't find tritip, you can use sirloin," I said. "That's what the original recipe calls for."

Jürgen dismissed my suggestion with a raised hand. "In Austria they use many substitutes such as *hueferscherzl, hueferschwanzl, wadlstutzen, gschnatter, schwarzes scherzl, weisses scherzl, duennes kuegerl and schalblattel.*"

"All excellent choices," I said with a straight face.

Alain looked at me, perplexed. I pulled him aside after Jürgen departed. "Have you given any thought to what will happen when the customers tonight pay with a credit card?"

"They must pay with cash."

"Americans don't carry cash. When they see we insist on cash, most of them will leave."

"But if they pay with the card," he said, "the money will go to an account controlled by Molinero. He relented to our plan, but he has not been here since the Sunday meeting. I do not like to say this, but I am not certain we can trust him."

"My nephew came with me this morning. He can reprogram the machine to a different account."

"This is legal?"

I shrugged. I had asked myself that question and given myself the same answer.

Alain thought about it briefly. "We are not stealing the money. We will use it to keep the restaurant alive."

"Yes, but we don't have time to set up a new bank account. We must use an existing one. My nephew set up the system that allows me to accept cards at my shop. We can use my account if you trust me."

"But of course," he responded. Then he thought for a moment. "Perhaps we should not tell the others."

I agreed, and Tristan went to work on the computer that served as a cash register and credit card processor. He had my account number and my bank's routing number, and in less than five minutes, the change had been made. I stood guard during the process, but it turned out to be unnecessary. The back-of-the-house staff were all in the kitchen, and the front-of-the-house staff had not yet arrived.

The usual pre-opening chaos set in around noon. I became the *garçon* again, this time joined by Tristan who demonstrated a knack for setting tables.

At ten minutes to six, I left the building through the loading dock and walked down the alley until I could see the entrance. Forty or fifty people were milling around. We were going to have a busy night.

What is it, I wondered, about Santa Fe? Are they really such avid restaurant goers that any opening draws a crowd? Are they merely curious about the concept of Austrian/Southwestern fusion? Do they have more money than sense?

Or are they just hungry?

When Wallace opened the doors at precisely six, her three assistants managed to be attentive and welcoming to each party they seated while at the same time doing so quickly enough that no one had a long wait. All twenty tables were occupied by six fifteen. As we saw them fill, Tristan and I rushed to the private dining area and dressed the four tables there. The last napkin had scarcely been inserted into its ring when Wallace showed a party of four to the back table.

"A special table for special people," she said, her voice as smooth and cold as Jell-O, but they loved it.

The seatings were smooth and the service speedy. Because of the *prix fixe* menu, most things were precooked. An order of *schnitzel con tres chiles* required merely placing the *schnitzel* on a warm plate, dousing it with the jalapeno sauce and spooning a portion of habañero relish on one side and poblanos *spätzle* on the other. When the kitchen staff saw how many orders were being placed, they started plating them up before the orders came in. There had been some concern that we had more staff than required, but the crowd was so large and the turnover so fast that Alain quickly grasped that enough had not been prepared. He ordered a third of the staff to plate, a third to deliver and the other third to start preparing more of everything. Tristan joined the wait staff and I tended bar, which, thankfully, consisted mostly of opening beer bottles and pouring wine for those who ordered it by the glass.

At one point, someone ordered a Rob Roy. I told the waitress who brought the order to tell the customer we were out of gin. She said a Rob Roy isn't made with gin, so I told her to change the excuse to we don't serve cocktails named after bandits. She gave me a funny look and left. I'm confident she had the good sense to make up a better excuse than the one I suggested, but I had neither the time nor the inclination to learn how to make a Rob Roy. Nor did I attempt to fill the orders for a Sex on the Beach or an Alabama

Slammer. Someone also ordered an Orgasm (presumably the name of a drink). I wondered if it was the same person who wanted sex on the beach.

I did manage scotch on the rocks, bourbon and coke and a martini. The latter was ordered very dry and delivered even drier because I couldn't find the vermouth. Despite the best efforts of the kitchen crew, demand eventually overwhelmed supply. The wait staff explained that the smoked trout appetizer was sold out. Soon the *schnitzel con tres chiles* was no longer available. The Linzer torte was crossed off the dessert menu. The smoked duck breast was sold out, followed by—to my surprise—the *tafelspitz Sangre de Cristo*.

By the time we closed the doors at shortly after ten, we had served 297 diners and taken in $10,325.56 in charges and tips, almost all of which was now residing in my bank account, a fact that was roiling my stomach.

Alain gathered everyone in the dining room, dragging Scruggs and his assistants out of the scullery against their protests that the pots should be scrubbed before having any meeting.

"When I told Molinero we had become a *compagnie*, it was mostly just blowing the air. I wanted him to know we are determined. Tonight, you saved me from making the false boast."

Idle boast, I thought to myself.

"We had a full house, and the customers liked the food. But we should remember how soon they disappeared after our opening as *Schnitzel*. Hubert Schuze is serving as the manager. He has an announcement for you."

"We are not in a position to pay anyone a salary. But Alain and I have decided the staff should be paid half of the gross revenue each night. The other half will go for supplies. This is a temporary plan, subject to change as we see how things go. Half of tonight's take is approximately five thousand dollars. There were twenty five people working tonight, so that is exactly two hundred dollars per person. Of course it is normal for a chef to make more than a waiter, a waiter to make more than a potscrubber, etc. I am not taking any pay, but I would like my expenses to be reimbursed at some point. Alain and I want you to agree on a plan for splitting the money. We will wait in the bar. After you decide, you need to do the usual cleaning. We will pay you at eleven in the morning. We will need all day to get ready if we have another night like tonight."

"How will you pay us?" asked Wallace Voile.

"In cash," I replied.

"But almost all the customers used credit cards. The money will not be available until the charges have cleared."

"I have made special arrangements for that," I said.

"Special arrangements?"

"Yes. Are there any other questions?"

Although she was glaring at me for ignoring her implied question of what the special arrangements were, she did so from a composed face.

Arliss Mansfield said, "I don't have a question, but I do have a request."

"Yes?"

He stood and turned to face the others. "I think we should give Alain and Hubie a round of applause."

They made it a robust round. Alain and I thanked them and retreated to the bar with Tristan. I opened a bottle of Gruet. I was certain it was better than the ginger ale I had brought.

Tristan opened a beer, Alain filled two coupes, and we toasted the evening. I usually drink Gruet from a flute, but the coupe was fun because the bubbles tickled my nose.

"Did you taste the food?" I asked.

"Of course. Nothing leaves my kitchen untasted."

"And?"

"The 'meat with crust', as Jürgen names it, is not to my taste. The sauce, however, is fresh and light. The beef dish is too complicated, but the ginger from the soda gives it a certain *Je ne sais quoi*. The *mole* deserves a star from *Michelin*. But it should not be pushed inside a potato dumpling."

"So these dishes will not be on the menu of your American food restaurant in France?"

"I am thinking the *mole* will be served over couscous."

We had closed the French doors but we could hear voices from the dining room, occasionally raised. Wallace Voile left two minutes into the meeting. Helen Mure stomped out after another ten. Shortly after that, the meeting broke up and the cleaning commenced.

Arliss Mansfield had been delegated to convey the plan they had agreed to. "I speak on behalf of the proletariat," he said with a smile. "We have voted for the first few days at least to give every worker an equal share."

Alain left. I suppose as *de facto chef de cuisine*, he wouldn't be expected to help clean. Tristan said he might as well pitch in, and I saw him enter the scullery. I sat at the bar with my Gruet in order not to be in the way of those doing the cleaning.

As I was finishing my second coupe, Maria Salazar brought me some toasted crusty bread slices spread with piñon and apricot pesto. The pesto had outlasted the trout. We shared the toast and champagne, the first food either of us had had for twelve hours.

We talked about the evening, speculating on what the future held for *Chile Schnitzel*. We talked about the food, about how the staff had rallied together, about their surprising decision to share the wealth.

"Power to the people," I said, and we made a mock toast.

"Well, most of them. Helen Mure walked out when it was clear we were going to vote equal shares," she said.

"I saw Wallace leave, too."

"That was odd," she said. "She left before we even got to the topic of pay. She didn't say a word. She just waited until the first person started talking and then quietly slipped away."

Maria had also been quietly slipping, but in my direction rather than away, scooting her stool closer to mine each time she reached for a piece of toast or lifted her coupe to sip the bubbly. We were now shoulder to shoulder at the bar. Like communist comrades.

But I wondered whether camaraderie was all she had in mind.

"Maybe Wallace wanted to celebrate our success with someone special," she suggested. "How about you, Hubie? Would you like to celebrate with me?"

"Uh . . ."

"I have some cold Gruet at my place."

What to do? At the risk of sounding presumptuous, I said, "I'm in a relationship."

She laughed. "You are so cute. Are you trying to tell me you're 'going steady'?"

"Well, uh . . ."

"You aren't married, are you?"

"No."

"Engaged?"

"No."

"Living with a woman?"

"No."

She stuck her hands on her hip. In a playful schoolmarmish voice, she said, "In a relationship with a man?"

I couldn't help laughing. "No."

"Well, in that case, I think it's probably safe for you to have a glass of champagne at my apartment."

She smiled at me. I smiled back.

I realized I didn't have to decide whether to accept or decline her offer. "I have to take Tristan home," I said.

47

I fortified myself with strong black coffee before approaching the reviews the next morning, jumping into the deep end by starting with Dagmar Mortensen. The headline was noncommittal—"*Herr Today, Gone Tomorrow?*"

> Readers of this column who believe my recent negative review of *Schnitzel* led to its closing give me too much credit. The food was bad enough to do that without my help.
>
> We were not surprised that *Schnitzel* closed. We are surprised that it reopened and astonished that it now claims to be Austrian/Southwestern fusion, a claim so outrageous as to require a second visit.
>
> The space still resembles Mad King Ludwig's Bavarian Castle, but with the word *Chile* added in front of the word *Schnitzel* in what appears to be a case of graffiti. Needless to say, my companion and I approached with trepidation.

The same lovely hostess showed us to the same impressive table setting. But after the napkins were pulled from their rings and laid across our laps, everything changed.

First, the menu is now *prix fixe*, an appetizer, entrée and dessert for only nineteen dollars. I chose the smoked trout with piñon and apricot pesto, a spectacular homage to our Land of Enchantment. The fish tasted like it had been swimming in the Chama that morning, and the piñon and apricot were equally fresh.

My companion selected the Caesar salad with *Verdolagas*, an overlooked green even among New Mexicans. I can only assume these were hothouse grown given the time of year, but they were crisp, tart, and delicious. The garlicky dressing had a Southwestern snap.

The *Gebratener Leberkäse* of my previous visit is nowhere to be found, heaven be praised. My entrée was the oddly named *schnitzel de tres chiles*, which featured perhaps the best jalapeno-flavored sauce I have ever tasted. The other *dos chiles* were a fiery *habañero* relish which was too hot to eat and a wonderful poblano infused *spätzle*.

My companion had the *tafelspitz Sangre de Cristo*, a dish I judged to be less successful than my *schnitzel de tres chiles*. However, it did have a subtle ginger undertone and a spicy horseradish sauce that worked well together. My companion actually preferred her dish to mine, so I am hesitant to denigrate the New Mexican version of *tafelspitz*.

Chile Schnitzel has wisely retained the desserts from their original menu, the sole addition being a *chipotle* sugar *crème brûlée* which may be the best dessert I have ever tasted.

The *Salzburger Nockerln* and *Linzer torte* were as good as

I remembered, but overshadowed by the magnificent *crème brûlée.*

I admit to being astonished that a restaurant that relied so heavily on fat, sugar and salt has managed to create a menu that captures the flavors of our region in new and inventive ways. My only concern is whether they will be able to sustain this new approach.

I shared her concern. Despite the relief—even elation—I felt after reading her review, I wondered what was next. A restaurant that serves only three appetizers and three entrées will fail when customers tire of those dishes, and I didn't think Austrian/Southwestern fusion offered many options beyond the few we had dreamt up.

I retrieved the five thousand dollars from my secret hiding place and took it to Santa Fe. After handing out the two-hundred-dollar shares, I had eight hundred dollars left over because Wallace Voile and her three assistants in the front of house crew had not shown up at eleven to claim their shares. Although we had agreed to use half of the proceeds for supplies, we had no proceeds at that point because the credit card charges had not cleared into my account.

Alain needed at least a few essentials, so I gave him the eight hundred, and he and Jürgen went shopping. I would just have to tell the front of house crew they would get paid the next day, a task I was dreading because they normally do not show up as early as the kitchen crew. It seemed unfair to tell them, in effect, that the check was in the mail simply because they had kept to their normal schedule. Still, we had said eleven for everyone. But when they weren't there by four, I began to worry less about telling them they wouldn't get paid and more about who was going to serve if they didn't show. I called Susannah and asked her to rustle up some help. She doesn't work the evening shift, and school was out for the Christmas break, so I knew she would be available. I was hoping a few of her co-workers would come along for some extra pay.

But the only co-workers she was able to bring were Kaylee and Arturo. She also roped in Tristan. Arturo took the bartending assignment off my hands. Susannah became the hostess, and Kaylee, Tristan and I became the wait staff. Because of Tristan's personality, he took to it naturally and raked in so many big tips that I felt guilty about the fact that tips were part of the shared revenue pool. Then I remembered I was working for free.

I figured being a waiter in a *prix fixe* restaurant would be easy. I mean, how hard is it to take the order, enter the order, go to the line when it is ready and take it to the table?

Turns out there is a bit more to it. Kaylee had been promoted from the pot scrubbing crew to the wait staff at *La Placita*, so she knew what she was doing. The same could not be said of Tristan and me. Susannah gave us a crash course before we opened. I can summarize it as serve from the left, clear from the right, put the main item of the entrée in the five o'clock position, bread and butter plates above the main meal plate, appetizer fork to the outside left, then the salad fork, the dinner fork, knife and spoon to the right, knife blade facing inward toward the dinner plate.

Simple, right? But I couldn't get the hang of it because everything happened so fast. The crowd was even larger than the first night, and I decided getting them their food was more important than the meat on the plate being at the right spot on an imaginary clock face.

When the diners had left and clean-up was over, Susannah held a review session.

"Two customers complained that your thumb was in their salad," she said to me rather sternly.

I held up my hands. "Impossible. Neither of my thumbs ever left my hands."

She did not laugh. "There is nothing worse than a thumb in the salad."

I resisted telling the joke about the waiter's finger in the soup. "Rafael puts too much salad on the plate," I said. "He needs to leave some space at the edge of the plate so you can hold it."

"You hold it from the bottom, Hubie." She handed a salad plate to Tristan, and he demonstrated with the plate resting on the tips of his fingers and thumb, all pointed upwards. I didn't appreciate my own nephew siding with my suddenly bossy friend.

"I didn't have time to carry one dish at a time," I said.

"Huh?"

"If I have one hand turned up like that, I can't pick up a second dish without using my thumb," I pointed out quite reasonably.

"You only hold the dish for the time it takes to move it from the tray to the table. Doing it one at a time doesn't slow you down."

"I didn't use a tray."

"Why not?"

"Because when I sat the tray down on its stand, it collapsed. So I decided just to carry the plates from the line to the tables, one in each hand."

"Good grief. It's just like a TV tray. You fold the legs open and then put the tray on it."

"I don't own a TV tray, so I don't know how to work them."

She stared at me. Then she gave me a big smile. "You're fired."

"Good," I said.

She turned to Tristan. "You are promoted to head waiter."

"Does that carry an increase in pay?"

"No," I chimed in. "We are on the Marxist system. Everyone gets two hundred a night."

"Except you," said Susannah.

"Except me," I agreed, but I couldn't remember why I had decided not to be paid. Probably because I didn't think I would be working. But being *garçon* and then bartender and now waiter was hard work.

"In that case," said Tristan, "I decline the promotion."

"But you're still willing to wait tables for us if our crew doesn't show up?" I asked him.

"Sure. The two hundred a night is good. But someone will have to provide transportation."

"You can ride with me," Susannah said, "but not tonight. I have a date with Ice."

She looked at me. "You can take him home, right?"

"Sure. But first I need to talk to you alone."

"I'll go see how the pot-washing is going," said Tristan.

After he left, I sat there for a moment as my palms dampened and my pulse elevated. My conscience told me I had to say something. I was trying out different wordings, searching for one that would put her on alert but not level any accusations.

"Jeez, Hubie, you look nervous. What is it?"

"I hope I'm doing the right thing by telling you this. I think Wallace Voile has been hitting on Rafael."

She fidgeted with her hair. "Has he responded?"

"Not that I know of."

"Do you think that has anything to do with why she didn't come to work?"

"I don't know. My guess would be no. Her colleagues didn't come to work either, so it must be something that involves all four of them."

She removed the elastic thing holding her hair, re-gathered it, and replaced the band. "You're not telling me this just because I criticized your waiter skills are you?"

We both laughed. Then she gave me a hug and left.

Three hundred twenty-one diners had spent $11,521.06 in charges and tips. The proceeds from the first night would clear in the morning. I could repay myself the five thousand dollar advance, pay the staff and have money left for supplies. What I could *not* do was continue making daily round-trips to Santa Fe to serve as the unpaid manager for *Chile Schnitzel*.

The job was not going to get easier. Deductions for federal and state income tax had to be taken from the employee's earnings. Their share of Social Security had to be deducted. The employer's share had to be calculated and remitted. Ditto for payments into the state's unemployment and workers compensation funds. A record had to be kept of income and expenses. Thus far all I had was a pocketful of receipts and a few scribbled notes. These were exactly the chores which had driven me from the accounting profession back in the eighties. Now I was in danger of becoming Barnaby the scrivener.

I wanted my life back. I wanted to awake in the morning with no place to go. I wanted to sit behind my counter and read, uninterrupted by anyone other than the occasional customer. I wanted to watch the stars from my patio in the evening. But most of all, I wanted the routine of the cocktail hour with Susannah.

If *Chile Schnitzel* succeeds, I thought to myself, they can hire a manager. If they fail, they won't need one. But what about the time between now and whenever it is that the place either sinks or swims? I thought about it driving back to Albuquerque. Unlike Douglas MacArthur, I vowed *not* to return.

"You want to be manager of *Chile Schnitzel*?" I asked Tristan.

I took his guffaw as a no.

48

The next morning was bitterly cold. I figured hell must have frozen over because that was the only circumstance under which I would be returning to *Chile Schnitzel.*

And I was in the Bronco doing just that. With five thousand dollars in a plastic bag. I had taken ten thousand out of my account and put half of it in my secret hiding place to repay myself for the money I had advanced to the restaurant. As long as I was getting out, I figured my money would want to tag along.

I had tried to stuff the other five thousand for *Chile Schnitzel* in my wallet, but I couldn't fold it like that, so I'd opted to be a bag man. I figured the label was apt since I was delivering money that had been laundered through my bank account.

It was well past eleven when I arrived, and a queue of those wishing to be paid formed quickly. Wallace and her crew were nowhere to be found.

"Same as yesterday," I said to Alain as I handed him the money.

"After paying everyone, you have eight hundred left over for supplies."

"That will do for now," he said, "but we are taught in the école de cuisine that the food is normally twenty-five percent of revenue. We are bringing in over ten thousand dollars each night, so we will need to spend at least twenty-five hundred a day, no?"

"But you spent only eight hundred yesterday, and there was enough food."

"*Oui.* But you forget that we are using food we had already on the hand. We cannot continue in this way."

"On hand," I corrected, "not 'on *the* hand'."

"And," he continued, "we have the eight hundred only because Ms. Voile and her associates were not here to be paid. We will have to pay them if they return. Or others if they do not."

I started to explain about the delayed cash flow from credit cards and strategies for building up cash reserves. Then I remembered my resolve not to get sucked in.

"Alain, I cannot continue to work here. I am happy the place is succeeding. I have high hopes that it will continue. But I have my own business to run."

He placed an arm around my shoulder.

"*Oui,* I understand. You have been our *garçon*, waiter and bartender. You were in those jobs—how should I say—*pas le meilleur.* But you were also our inspiration, and in that job you were *supérieur.*"

He agreed to serve as manager. I agreed to be on call for any questions. We agreed that he would dispatch someone to pick up the money they would continue to deposit in my account until they set up their own bank account. If the Israelis and Palestinians agreed as much as we did, peace would descend upon the Middle East.

"What about Molinero?" I asked.

"He has disappeared. Perhaps he and Voile have run away to the south of France," he said with a smile on his face.

Eventually, Molinero had to be involved. Despite the fact that the ship was in the hands of the mutineers, it still belonged to the crown. Or in this case, the investors. We didn't even know who they were. Then again, maybe Molinero had gone forward with the bankruptcy filing as planned. I thought it would be a sad irony if the *gens d'armes* seized the restaurant when it was at the height of its success. But these were things I had to stop thinking about. It was not my concern.

Susannah, along with Tristan and Kaylee, showed up at four. Arturo could not get time off from *La Placita*. The three of them began to ready the dining area. Shortly before six, I heard shouts and chants from outside and mused that we were perhaps going to attract a rowdy crowd, it being a Friday.

But when I opened the doors at six, I saw Wallace Voile and her crew carrying pickets that read, "Unfair to workers." Some diners ignored them and came in, but others were talking to them and hesitating.

I wanted to discuss it with Susannah, but she was too busy. So was Rafael, but he had the initial tranche of appetizers ready on the line, so I told him he had to talk to Voile and find out why they were picketing.

I watched their conversation from the door trying to read their body language since I was too distant to hear their verbal one. They appeared to be engaged in a lovers' spat, although maybe I was reading that in based on what I had previously seen.

Rafael looked dejected as he returned, and it was obvious that what he told me was not the truth. Or at least not the whole truth.

"She says they are concerned they are not being paid."

"But we are paying everyone. All they have to do is show up and collect."

"I told her that, but she said a cash payment is not professional. They want a pay stub showing payments to Social Security, workers comp, things like that."

"Why didn't they discuss it with us before picketing? We plan to do those things as soon as possible."

He shrugged. "I have to get back to work."

Arliss and Barry making threats. M'Lanta and Arliss skulking around the premises. Wallace and Rafael fawning over each other and neither acknowledging the other in any other way. Kuchen and Molinero disappearing. Raoul Deschutes warning me to keep silent. Mure and Salazar fighting or flirting. Or both. The wait staff going on strike. *Chile Schnitzel* had more threats, jealousies, and intrigues than Raymond Chandler's *The Big Sleep*. And neither one of them had a plot I could follow.

I went to the men's room. There was a sign that read, "Employees must wash their hands prior to returning to work." How about, "Employees must wash their hands of working here?" I said out loud.

That was what I vowed—again—to do. But since I was there and no one else was available to do it, I tended bar again. It was less hectic than being a waiter on Thursday, but more hectic than being a bartender on Wednesday because the diners were thanking God it was Friday.

I never use a corkscrew because wine tastes to me like champagne gone flat. But I had mastered the art the first night I served as bartender because I had to open some bottles when wine was ordered by the glass. You might suppose a professional bar would have one of those fancy corkscrews with levers and gears that practically pull the corks out by themselves. But the only one I could find was like a miniature auger, a wooden handle with a spiral-threaded piece attached. I couldn't push it down hard enough to make it bite while I turned it. So I held the handle with my right hand and delivered a blow to the top with my left fist. With the point thusly driven in, turning the handle produced the desired effect.

It was a good thing I'd been able to practice that maneuver on Wednesday because on Friday we had a pinot grigio kind of crowd.

Then someone ordered an entire bottle of cheap chardonnay from South Africa. When I struck the corkscrew, it sank about an inch into the bottle. Must be the softest cork in history, I thought to myself. But despite turning the screw vigorously enough to conjure up the ghost of Henry James, nothing happened. I tried reversing to see if the screw would disengage. It just wobbled. Finally, I yanked it out in frustration and discovered the problem. There was no cork.

A wine bottle with a tin screw cap. Who knew? I screwed off the cap and had it ready for Kaylee when she returned. She gave it a funny look but took it away.

Susannah came to the bar a few minutes later to inform me that wine is always uncorked at the table, not by the bartender.

"*Chateau Apartheid* cannot be uncorked at the table because it has no cork," I explained quite reasonably.

"It doesn't matter whether it has a cork or a cap," she responded. "Wine is always *opened* at the table."

"Why?"

She rolled her eyes. "So the customer can see the bottle and be sure it hasn't been opened."

I didn't see what difference that made. It has to be opened before you can drink it, so why does it matter where that happens? But I could see she was in no mood to debate the irrationality of restaurant protocol, so I said, "In this case, the customer would not have liked what he saw. The tin cap had a big hole in it."

"Oh my God! You served wine with a defective top? It could make someone sick."

"It didn't have a defective top."

"You said it had a hole in it."

"Yes, and I put it there."

She gave me a blank look.

"I was trying to open it with the corkscrew," I explained.

She showed me how to spot a tin cap, which only made my work more difficult because I had to examine the neck of each bottle before deciding to twist or screw. That sounds lewd, but you know what I mean.

Despite such hardships, I survived my final shift behind the mahogany. It helped that I was sipping Gruet during the slow moments, of which there were precious few. But I did manage to work in enough sips to finish the bottle.

By rough estimate, I figured *Chile Schnitzel* had done as well on Friday as it had the first two nights. I wasn't going to total it up or worry what to do with it, but I was happy for my friends' success.

I was cleaning up the bar when Maria brought a *crème brûlée*.

"The last one. I hid it when I saw they were running low. Want to share it with me?"

"Sure. Shall I open a split of Gruet?" I said, referencing our lunch at *La Casa Sena*.

She gave me a radiant smile. "Half bottles are for work days."

She evidently recalled that afternoon as accurately as did I.

The velvety *crème*, the spicy *brûlée* topping and the icy champagne were an even better trio than Athos, Porthos and Aramis. Contrary to popular belief, D'Artagnan was not one of the three. I mentioned the three tastes of the *crème brûlée* to Maria and proposed a toast, "*Tous pour un, un pour tous.*" As soon as I said it, I wondered if my newfound compulsion to use every French phrase I'd ever heard would subside once I left the restaurant business.

"To Alexandre Dumas," she added. Beauty and brains.

Maria had brought only one spoon. We shared that and a single flute. Some guys are quick to notice when a woman flirts with them. Many men pick up on it even before it actually happens because they assume they are irresistible to women.

I am not one of those guys. My natural inclination has always been to assume an inverse relationship between how desirable a woman is and the likelihood she will be interested in me. So I am often the last to know when I am being flirted with.

But I was beginning to believe that Maria Salazar was doing exactly that. Worse, I was beginning to hope she was. Worse because I didn't know what to do. Well, what else was new?

"I see Tristan is here again. Do you have to take him home tonight?"

"No," I said, my voicing cracking like a thirteen-year-old. "He's riding with Susannah."

"I still have that cold Gruet at my place," she said, "and another special treat I think you'll like."

The walk to her apartment on East Alameda took only ten minutes. It was a small one bedroom with brick floors and a kiva fireplace in which she lit a piñon fire. She served cheesecake with a chocolate sauce you knew on first taste was made by a professional *saucier*. I wondered if that was the special treat.

The Gruet was icy cold. The fire was warm. Maria did not look like a woman who had worked in a hot kitchen all day. She did smell of food, but it was a pleasant scent mixed with her sandalwood perfume.

"You don't really want to drive back to Albuquerque tonight, do you?"

"No. I'm too tipsy."

"Would you like to stay here tonight?"

"Sure. I'd be happy to sleep on this sofa."

"It's not a sofa, Hubie. It's a love seat. You know what that means?"

I thought maybe "It means you make love on it" was the answer she was fishing for, but I also thought saying so would be too bold, so I said, "What does it mean?"

She tilted her head to an alluring angle and moistened her lips with her tongue before answering. "It means it's not long enough to sleep on." Then she giggled.

"I'm not very tall. I bet I can fit."

She leaned in close to me, her lips only inches from mine. "Try it."

I wasn't sure what I was to try, but I opted for trying to fit on the love seat. I snugged my head against one arm of the love seat and swung my legs up. They reached over the other arm by several inches.

"I told you you wouldn't fit."

"Well, I can sleep on the floor."

"The floor is brick. Pretty to look at. Too hard to sleep on. You'll have to sleep in the bed."

"What about you? You're as tall as I am. You can't sleep on the love seat either."

"I'll have to sleep in the bed, too."

"Oh."

"Is that okay with you?"

I hoped my gulp wasn't audible.

Her eyes were the color of freshly brewed tea, her lashes long and curled. I stared into those lovely eyes until they blurred because she was too close for me to focus. Or because I had enjoyed too much Gruet. But a blurry Maria was as alluring as a clear one.

"Wait here," she said.

The last thing I heard was the sound of a shower running.

49

Susannah was giving me a well-deserved roasting, and we were both laughing as she did so.

"Men are supposed to fall asleep *after* sex, Hubie, not before."

As you may have guessed, I had awoken that morning under a blanket on Maria's love seat. My location and the fact I had slept in my clothes made me suspect no hanky had been panked. I hoped that—other than falling asleep on her love seat—I had done nothing further to make a fool of myself.

"So what happened to your principle of not dating two women at the same time?"

"I didn't have a date with Maria."

"Right. And Clinton 'never had sex with that woman'."

I sighed. "Neither did I. She invited me to her apartment for a late night snack. Then, seeing that I was too tipsy to drive back to Albuquerque, she graciously invited me to spend the night."

"In her bed."

"Yes."

"With her in it."

"The love seat was too—"

"I know, the love seat was too short for either one of you to sleep on, so you were going to share the bed strictly for convenience. Maybe she was planning to put one of those bundling boards in the bed between you."

I sighed again, a sigh of what might have been. "An unnecessary precaution, as it turned out. God, I can't believe I fell asleep."

"Admit it, Hubie. You knew exactly what she had in mind, and you were looking forward to it."

"I wasn't absolutely certain."

"But you wouldn't have resisted once she got you in bed."

"Probably not."

"So you *will* date two women at the same time."

"It wasn't a date."

"Okay, so you won't date two women at the same time, but you will have sex with two at the same time."

"No way. That's way too kinky for me."

"You know what I mean."

She was right, of course. I was ready and willing to jump into bed with Maria. Well, willing anyway.

"The weird thing is I feel guilty even though Dolly said she isn't the jealous type and doesn't care what I do when we aren't together."

"That's because it doesn't matter what Dolly thinks about it. It's *your* rule you would be violating, not hers. She can't give you permission to break your own rule. Only you can do that."

She was right again. I needed to forget what Dolly said and decide what I believed. I figured I had plenty of time to do that. After last night, I didn't think I'd be invited back to Maria's apartment, much less to her bed.

So I signaled Angie for a second round and asked Susannah about her date with Rafael after the Wednesday re-opening.

"You're a good friend, Hubie."

"I am?"

"Yeah. I know it wasn't easy for you to tell me about Rafael and Wallace, but you wanted to protect me, and I think that's very sweet."

"Aw, shucks."

Angie brought our second round and more chips. "Turns out I didn't have to ask him. He brought it up."

Damn, I thought. He jilted her. That's why she called him Rafael for the first time. It signals a change in their relationship. Why does such a great young woman have such bad luck with men? It isn't fair.

"You were right," she said. "She had been coming on to him. He said he played along because he didn't want to risk offending her. He seems to think she's dangerous somehow."

I hoped that was true. Not the part about Wallace being dangerous. The part about him just playing along.

"I don't doubt it." I said. "Machlin Masoot told me to be careful what I said to her. Did Rafael say why he thinks she's dangerous?"

"Only that she seemed to wield a lot of power when they were at Café Alsace together. Two employees who didn't get along with her were fired."

"So is she still after him?"

"I don't think so. When she first came on to him, he figured he could play along until he got a sense of whether the place was going to survive. I guess you could say he was playing for time. But when he talked to her on the picket line, she had reverted to her normal cold fish persona."

Something told me that wasn't the whole story. I thought about it while I sipped. "The last time we were here, you *proved* Wallace killed Barry Stiles." The italics were for Susannah, who smiled at me making fun of her. "If memory serves, the clues were that she's using an alias, she worked at Café Alsace with Barry, and she's the perfect villain because she is so unlikely. So how does coming on to Rafael then picketing the place then giving him the cold shoulder fit with your theory of Voile as murderess?"

She was still smiling. She loves mysteries. "I remember Nero Wolfe saying you should never call a woman Jew a Jewess, but it's okay to call a woman murderer a 'murderess'."

"Who is Nero Wolfe?"

"He was a hugely fat detective who raised orchids and never left his house."

"Must be hard to detect without leaving the house."

"He used logic. You don't have to leave the house to use logic."

"I suppose he's fictional."

"You can learn a lot reading fiction." She scooped up some salsa.

"So?" I prompted.

"So what?"

"So how does the new information about Voile fit into your theory?"

"She walked out of the meeting where pay was going to be decided. She didn't even bother to show up the next day to collect her share. Then on the next day, pay is suddenly so important to her that she's picketing about it. It doesn't make sense, does it?"

I shook my head. "Nothing at *Chile Schnitzel* makes sense."

50

I wanted to spend an evening alone for a change.

I love books but don't have room for them. I either check them out from the library or buy them, read them and give them away. On my shelf that evening was the unabridged edition of the Oxford English Dictionary which should come with a hydraulic lift for hoisting it up to a table where it can be opened. Alongside it were a New Mexico atlas and a first edition of *Pueblo Pottery Making: A Study at the Village of San Ildefonso* by Carl E. Guthe, published by Harvard in 1925. I've read it twice and keep it because it's too valuable to give away.

So I went back to Escoffier and discovered he had a dark side.

When he wasn't engaged in humanitarian efforts such as banning the practice of beating apprentices, he was swindling money from his employer.

While in charge of the kitchens at the Savoy, Escoffier received a five percent commission—also known as a kick-back—from his suppliers. In addition, some of the tradesmen testified that it was common knowledge that "large presents consisting of packages of goods were sent every week addressed to a Mr. Boots, Southsea." Some have speculated that Escoffier, who lived apart from his wife and children, had a second family in Southsea. He took dating two women at once to a higher level than I ever imagined.

In 1900, Escoffier signed a confession admitting to fraud. No charges were brought, however, perhaps because the famous hotel would rather eat the loss than suffer the scandal. As I contemplated what to have for dinner, I thought of a meal Escoffier had described in his memoir.

> Our dinner that evening consisted of a cabbage, potato, and kohl-rabi soup, augmented with three young chickens, an enormous piece of lean bacon, and a big farmhouse sausage. To follow, we were served with a leg of mutton, tender and pink, accompanied by a puree of chestnuts. Then, a surprise—but one which was not entirely unexpected from our host, who had an excellent cook—an immense, hermetically sealed terrine, which, placed in the middle of the table, gave out, when it was uncovered, a marvelous scent of truffles, partridges, and aromatic herbs. This terrine contained eight young partridges, amply truffled and cased in fat bacon, a little bouquet of mountain herbs and several glasses of fine-champagne cognac. All had been lengthily and gently cooked in hot embers. At the same time was served a celery salad. As for the wines, we had first the excellent local wine, then Burgundy, and finally a famous brand of champagne. The dinner ended with beautiful local fruit, and fine liqueurs.

Just reading about it made me queasy. I'm not a vegetarian, but I admit to being bothered by the fact that a single meal had required the supreme sacrifice of three young chickens, a pig, and eight young partridges. No mention was made of a pear tree. They also ate a leg of mutton. I don't know what a mutton is, but I assume it must be killed before its leg can be eaten. Or maybe it can hobble around on three legs awaiting the next grand repast.

I settled on simpler fare, roasted poblanos with queso fresco and a glass of ice cold Tecate.

Even though it was just above freezing, I opened the doors to the patio before retiring. I wrapped myself in the covers like a mummy and slept the sleep of the blissfully ignorant.

51

I had planned to follow the evening of solitude with a morning of more of the same, so I was irritated by the philistine pounding on my door at nine the next morning.

Pulling the covers over my head didn't work. The pounder was persistent, and Geronimo was howling after each knock. Blam, awrwooo, blam, awrwooo. When the knocker heard the howls, he beat louder, scaring Geronimo into whelping less noisily. The two of them created an interesting syncopation, but they lacked melody altogether, so I soon grew tired of the music. I went to the door to see Whit Fletcher. At least Danny Duran wasn't with him.

Fletcher held in his meaty hand a paper that looked disturbingly like the warrant he'd brought on his previous visit.

I stared down at it. "Duran didn't get another warrant to arrest me for killing Barry Stiles, did he?"

"Nope. This here is a *subpoena duces tecum.* You've been charged with larceny." He put on his reading glasses. "This *subpoena* orders you to appear in court next Thursday and bring all personal and business bank statements for the last two months as well as records of credit card transactions of any and all accounts, both personal and commercial." He looked up at me. "What the hell you been up to, Hubert?"

I guessed I now had an answer to Alain's question about whether it was legal for me to reroute the credit card charges to my bank account. But I hadn't taken any of the money, so I didn't think I was guilty of larceny. I knew we must have studied larceny in my accounting classes, but I couldn't remember exactly what it was.

"I've been running a restaurant. What's larceny?"

He looked back at the *subpoena*. "It says here, 'larceny, by New Mexico statute, is the trespassory taking and asportation of the tangible personal property of another with the intent permanently to deprive him of its possession'."

"What do 'trespassory' and 'asportation' mean?"

"My guess is that 'trespassory' probably has something to do with trespassing, and 'asportation' is probably a fancy way of saying 'transportation'. Which means in good old English that you trespassed on someone's property and took something away when you left. Probably that restaurant you just mentioned. Want to tell me about it?"

No, I didn't. I signed a paper acknowledging receipt of the *subpoena* and took Geronimo for his morning walk.

52

"Trespassory taking and asportation of personal property? Is that different from theft?"

The day had passed about as quickly as the accretion of stalagmites. I spent most of it pacing because I couldn't concentrate on anything else. I just wanted five o'clock to arrive so I could discuss my problem with Susannah.

"There must be some technical difference," I said. "Otherwise, why have two crimes, theft and larceny?"

"It's the legal system. Why have 'trespassory' and 'asportation'?"

"Good point. You don't think I could actually be convicted, do you? I didn't keep any of the money. I gave it all to the restaurant."

"No, Hubert, you did not give it all to the restaurant. You gave some of it to the employees."

"But it was their pay for working there."

"Authorized by whom?"

"Molinero. He asked for a show of hands. After almost everyone voted for the plan, he wished us luck. He approved keeping the place open."

"But did he approve paying the employees?"

I rubbed my temples. A headache was bearing down on me as I recalled the meeting. "He said there was no money to pay us, and everyone agreed to work without pay."

"So you took restaurant money that should have gone to Molinero or the investors, and you used it to pay your friends."

"They are not my friends." I drank some of my margarita. "Well, some of them are." I took another sip. "You know what's really weird? I was reading last night about Escoffier embezzling money and supplies from the Savoy hotel, and I find out the very next day that I've been doing the same thing."

"What did Escoffier do with the stuff he took?"

"Evidently he used some of it to support his mistress in Seaside."

A mischievous smile crept across her lips. "And you gave some of it to your mistress."

"Maria is not my mistress. We've never so much as kissed."

"Try telling that to the judge when it comes out you spent the night in her apartment."

I signaled for Angie.

"Your glass is half full," said Susannah.

"It feels half empty," I said, "like me."

I asked Angie to bring me some aspirin. I know you're not supposed to take medicine with alcohol, but it sure is easier to wash it down with a margarita than with a glass of water.

"I can't believe this is happening to me."

"It's the restaurant syndrome, Hubie."

"Restaurant syndrome? I've never heard of it."

"Maybe you know it by its original name, *le syndrome de restaurant.*"

I groaned. "Please, no more French words and phrases."

"But that's it. That's the syndrome. You start working in a restaurant, and you have to learn all those French terms. It begins to affect your thinking, like the twins thing."

"The twins thing?"

"Yeah. You know, like how twins have this special language that makes it easy for them to communicate with each other, but it messes them up when they try to deal with normal people. Restaurant workers are like that. We may start out normal, but after you begin using words like *prix fixe, hors d'oeuvres, à la carte, escargots* and *raison d'être*, you get a little crazy."

"*Raison d'*être?"

"I think it's a raisin soufflé."

"No. I think the phrase for a raisin soufflé is *au courant.*"

"Anyway," she continued, "it affects your judgment, and pretty soon you're doing crazy things like actually eating snails because you think of them as escargots and don't realize they're just slimy snails. And the next thing you know, you're funneling money from the restaurant to your personal account."

"I didn't 'funnel money'. I was just trying to keep the place in business."

"I could see the changes come over you, Hubie. I noticed it when you called me up there to waitress. You weren't yourself. Taking charge, showing leadership, inventing dishes."

"Thanks a lot."

She laughed. "Admit it, that is not exactly you."

"You're right. But I really invented only one dish, the *schnitzel con tres* chiles. Rafael invented all three appetizers. Even Miss Gladys contributed with *Tafelspitz Sangre de Cristo.*"

"I can't imagine what Alain thought about that one."

"He said it had a certain *Je ne sais quoi.*"

"See. There you go again with the French. I hear that all the time. What does it mean?"

"I don't know what."

"Really? I thought you would know."

"I do know. It means I don't know what."

"If you don't know what, how can you say you know what it means?"

I raised my glass. "*To le syndrome de restaurant.*"

53

"Larceny."

Layton Kent puffed the word out like a smoke ring, closing his mouth behind it lest it should float back on him. "Unsavory," he said.

"I'm innocent."

He peered out over what must surely have been the largest martini glass in the world. The curve of its flared cone rose almost a foot from the thin base.

"All my clients are innocent, Hubert." He gave me a thin smile. "And when they are not, I make them so."

The waiter had brought the glass straight from the freezer. The frost evaporated while the gin and vermouth were stirred.

"No olive?" I asked after the waiter departed.

Kent's stare conveyed his disdain of olives. We were at his table overlooking the eighteenth hole. The golf course was beautiful with its rolling contours and assortment of deciduous trees, few of which were native to New Mexico. Their leaves were gone, of course, it being December. The grass was yellow. The tawny scene was relieved by the green piñon and ponderosa pines. The sun had warmed the air enough that the scenery was despoiled by old gentlemen in stretch-waist pants being pushed to their limits. Both the men and the pants. I recalled that Will Rogers said, "Long ago, when men cursed and beat the ground with sticks, it was called witchcraft. Today it's called golf."

The three ounces of gin and one ounce of vermouth looked lost in the flower-vase-sized glass. Maybe the idea was to make the portion seem abstemious. He took a sip, placed the glass on the table and read the papers I'd brought.

"As I have come to expect, you acted incautiously, but not feloniously. The prosecution will no doubt attempt to represent that diversion of the proceeds to the staff was unlawful enrichment, a claim without which they have no case. However, the investors could have harbored no hope of gain had Molinero closed the restaurant as he planned to do. Thus, keeping it open did not damage the investors, and had the possibility of benefitting them." He looked up at me. "There is, however, one problem. Looking at the numbers you have presented me, five thousand dollars seems to be missing."

"I took five thousand dollars out of the ten I took to Santa Fe on Friday because I had used five thousand of my own money to pay the staff on Thursday."

"Why?"

"Because the credit card charges we took in on Wednesday needed to clear, so I made an advance to the restaurant."

"But there is no indication of a withdrawal of five thousand dollars from either of your bank accounts on any of those days."

"That's because I didn't get it from the bank. I had at my house."

His eyes widened slightly. "You had five thousand dollars in cash at your house?"

"Yes."

"Where?"

"In my secret hiding place."

"Where did the money come from?" He held up a palm before I could answer. "If the money was from an illegal source, do not answer my question."

"It wasn't illegal. It was from the sale of an old Laguna pot."

"Was the buyer given a receipt?"

Oops. "No. I was in Santa Fe. Tristan was tending the shop."

"Was the buyer known to him?"

"No. Is this going to be a problem?"

He took a sip of his martini, then closed his eyes and seemed to be daydreaming. But I've seen that pose before and realize that Layton never daydreams. "You did make an entry into your revenue log of the five thousand as soon as you returned from Santa Fe and learned that your nephew had made the sale."

"Well, it was sort of hectic going back and forth to—"

"That was not a question, Hubert. It was a statement that you *did* make an entry into your revenue log of the five thousand as soon as you returned from Santa Fe and learned that your nephew had made the sale."

"Oh. Right. I did."

"And you dated it properly."

"Yes."

"And you put the money in your store safe."

"Actually, I put it in—"

"Your store safe."

"Right," I said.

"Very good. 'Secret hiding place' is not a phrase one wants to utter in court. You do understand what *duces tecum* means, do you not?"

I started to say it sounded like a pair of twos had won a poker hand, but remembered Layton's sense of humor. Or, more accurately, his lack thereof.

"Make sure you bring all the records," he directed. "And make sure all the things you have told me today are in them."

The waiter arrived and asked Layton if the gentleman would be joining him for lunch. I looked at the entrance to see if someone was waiting for permission to come to Layton's table. Then I realized the gentleman was me. Or I.

I guess if I were truly a gentleman, I would have known which pronoun to use.

Layton shook his head, and I left.

54

The hearing on Thursday was brief and my participation even briefer.

It felt like the meeting of some secret society like the Masons or Skull and Bones. I figured it would be in a big courtroom, but we were in a small hearing room instead. A guard of some sort stood by the door and another one next to another door behind a raised desk which I assumed was probably called a bench. They wore sidearms. I couldn't imagine why. Aside from the two guards, there were only five people in the room, a young lady named Rincon from the District Attorney's Office, her assistant, Layton, one of his paralegals and me. None of us looked like violent felons, although Ms. Rincon did wear a rather stern expression which became positively severe when I smiled at her.

The guard next to the bench yelled, "All rise."

The judge was a wizened little fellow with stringy hair and a face full of broken veins. He eyed the two steps to the bench as if they were the north face ascent to Everest. After perhaps twenty seconds during which he seemed to be debating whether to make the climb, he hiked up his robe with his left hand, placed his right one on the bench for support and slowly mounted the steps.

He took his chair and mumbled for us to be seated. Then he directed Layton and Rincon to approach the bench. They whispered among themselves for ten minutes, but I wouldn't have understood them even had they been audible because they were speaking legalese.

My nerves had begun to fray that morning when I put on my suit. Nothing good ever happens when you're wearing a suit. Now I was in a room being guarded by two guys with guns, and an aged drunk was going to decide my fate based on a conversation which, for all I knew, was an example of speaking in tongues.

I was beginning to hyperventilate. The phrase, 'the wheels of justice', sprang to mind. I remembered the saying that those wheels grind exceedingly slow. I felt like I was being dragged into that mill to be ground up, like corn being ground into meal between two heavy stones.

Then, out of the miasma of irrational dread came a flicker of reason. I focused on it until it brightened into the light of understanding. I knew who killed Barry Stiles and I knew why. I figured the killer had an accomplice. I had a hunch who it was but wasn't certain. I feared others might be in danger.

55

The judge took the matter under advisement. Layton asked that I be allowed to remain out of custody and under my own recognizance. Ms. Rincon made no objection. Maybe smiling at her was not a mistake.

I almost wished I'd been sent to jail so that I wouldn't have had to get up at five the next morning and drive to Santa Fe.

I parked a few blocks away so that no one would see the Bronco near the restaurant. I was happy to find the locks had not been changed. The building was quiet and dark, but I tiptoed around just to make certain I was alone. I would have embarked on this mission after leaving court, but I knew the place would be full of staff preparing for the dinner rush. There were too many late night callers to try it under cover of darkness. Early morning is definitely the best time to do a B & E at a restaurant. No one is ever around. Susannah had told me once that B & E is what they call breaking and entering in detective fiction. I had even learned how to loid a lock from a mystery she insisted I read.

That wouldn't work on the door I wanted to open. Its deadbolt could be moved only with a key. But the top half of the door had a window through which I had seen Molinero sitting at his desk the day I sought his approval of my charger design and asked him how he kept his office so clean because I wondered what Scruggs was doing in the office and how he had gained entry.

I knew how I was going to gain entry—through that window. Not a good method if you wanted to conceal the break-in, but I had no reason to do that. I wasn't entering as a thief. I was looking for evidence. If I found any, I was planning to carry it away in my brief case. But first I would have to make room for it by removing the roll of duct tape, the two suction cups, and the glass cutter. You can probably figure out what I did with the window, so I won't bother to spell it out for you.

I had never done it before, but it worked perfectly. I carried the taped glass by the two suction cups and placed it on one of the work stations. I lifted a chair through the space where the pane had been and put it down on the office side of the door. I placed a second chair on my side of the door and stood on it. I lifted one leg through the window and down onto the inside chair. Then I bent forward and swung my torso to the inside. I was now straddling the bottom of the window with one foot on each chair.

There was, of course, a half-inch ridge of glass around the opening because the cutter wouldn't snug up completely against the frame. I had coated that ridge liberally with duct tape to avoid performing an accidental vasectomy during this part of the operation.

Had I been even an inch taller, I don't think I could have made it. But once my body was on the office side, the rest was easy. I brought my other leg through and stepped down to the office floor.

I spent the next hour going through Molinero's desk. I found a set of books and—for the first time—gave thanks for having studied accounting. After examining the ledgers, I realized there had to be another set of books. But they were not in the desk.

I walked to the safe and eyed its massive door. Loiding was even less of an option than it had been with the double cylinder door lock. Nor was there a window to cut. I wondered if I could drill the lock out. Go to a hardware store, purchase a huge electric drill with some sort of hardened steel bit or maybe one covered with diamonds and just drill through the door. I quickly dismissed that idea. Using dynamite was dismissed even more quickly. If I detonated enough dynamite to open that safe, I'd have to be a mile away with a remote control in order not to blow myself to bits.

A crazy thought came to me—maybe it was open. I grasped the big handle and pulled. I pushed it up and down. Well, I did say it was a crazy idea.

I moved the dial ever so slightly and listened for a click. I don't know why. It just seemed like something to try. I got down on my knees and put my ear to the metal. I rotated the dial slowly through each of its numbers. The only thing I heard was the waves-hitting-the-beach noise you hear when you cover your ear. I stared at the safe and thought about Bing Crosby. He died when I was in my early teens, but I'm a fan of the music of my parents' generation—the era of crooners and big bands. I remembered a line from one of his songs:

A sentimental crook
With a touch that lingers
In his sandpapered fingers

The sentimental crook was Jimmy Valentine, the safecracker immortalized by William Sydney Porter in a short story titled, *A*

Retrieved Reformation. Valentine's sandpapered fingers were so sensitive he could feel the clicks that revealed the combination as he turned the tumblers.

I rubbed my fingers against the low loop carpet. Not exactly sandpaper, but it did make them feel sensitive. I laid my hand gently on the dial and turned it slowly. I felt nothing. What an idiot I am, I said to myself. If people could open safes that easily, what would be the purpose of having one? You can't loid or drill or sandpaper-finger your way in. You have to have the combination.

I was famished. I'm not used to skipping breakfast. I returned to the kitchen by reversing the moves I had used to pass through the window into the office. I found some sautéed beef tips and microwaved them. There were no tortillas, so I put the beef between two slices of bread. I found a white plastic tub labeled *jalapeños* and took it and the sandwich back to the office. I slipped through the window with ease. Having mastered the moves, I could now do it even with a sandwich in one hand and a plastic tub in the other.

Unfortunately, the tub turned out to contain just jalapeño juice. The actual chiles were gone. I took a sip. I liked it. It had the fiery burn of jalapeños. But it was useless because pouring it on the sandwich would make the bread soggy. The sandwich was too plain and dry to eat. After a few bites, I rolled it in a paper napkin and tossed it in the trash.

I looked for the combination. It wasn't on a piece of tape stuck under a drawer. It wasn't in Molinero's daily planner. It wasn't in his files under 'C' for combination. I went back through the books looking for numbers that had nothing to do with accounting. I went through his rolodex and found some numbers that weren't in telephone format. One read Hansen Wholesale #4952. There was a three-hole punch with the number 234332 taped underneath. I arranged the numbers I'd found into possible safe combinations: 23-43-32, 4-9-5-2, 2-5-9-4, and so forth. I tried all the combinations and permutations I could think of. In the back of my mind, I knew I was on a fool's errand, but irrational hope kept whispering to me.

The next voice I heard was not whispering. "What do you think you're doing?"

I turned to see Molinero glaring at me though the window.

"I was checking to see if the safe was open," I temporized. "Fortunately, it's not, so I guess whoever broke in wasn't able to get into the safe."

A slight furrowing of the brow indicated he might buy it, so I continued. "I came back to see if I could find my watch, but when I came in, I saw your window glass had been removed. My first thought was a break-in. But maybe you're just having new glass installed."

I know it was lame, but it was the best I could do on the spur of the moment.

He shook his head. "I don't think so."

He unlocked the door and pushed it open. It swung back towards the frame but did not quite close. He walked to the desk and looked down at his open ledger.

"Why were you looking at my books?"

"I wasn't," I said in a voice that even I didn't believe. "Like I said, I saw the—"

"Yeah, yeah. You saw the window gone and wanted to check the safe. And you came to look for your missing watch when no one was here."

He reached into his jacket and came out with a gun. I don't know anything about guns, but I knew everything I needed to know about this one; namely, it was pointed at me.

"Sit down," he ordered, motioning with the gun barrel toward his office chair.

I sat.

He looked at me and laughed. "You of all people. I knew there was a risk someone would figure it out, but not you. Never you. You know nothing about restaurants. How did you do it? How did you figure it out?" I tried to make a hasty calculation. Should I continuing to play the innocent or should I admit I had figured it out? Which would make him less likely to use that gun?

"You made a mistake," I said.

"What was it?"

"When you left my shop that first day, you said, 'You won't regret this, Mr. Schuze'."

"So?"

"You introduced yourself as Santiago Molinero, but all I said to you was, 'I'm Hubert, but people generally call me Hubie'. Yet you called me by my last name as you left."

"So? I could have known your last name before I entered the place."

"Obviously, you did know it. But you pretended you needed to use the bathroom and picked my shop only because it was empty."

He seemed to be weighing options. "You did look at the books, right?"

I nodded.

"And?"

"They are strictly on the up and up," I said.

"But you knew there had to be another set. That's why you were trying to open the safe."

"Don't be ridiculous," I said with more bluster than I felt. "There's no way I could open that safe. Why would I even try?"

"Because you're a dreamer and a fool."

That stung, even considering the source.

"I *did* know who you were," he said with a cocky expression on his face. "I knew a lot about you. You were almost perfect for my purposes. I could run up expenses by having you make special chargers. And you've been charged with murder before, so I figured if I had to get rid of anyone, your record would make you a good suspect, especially if I used one of your glazing chemicals for rodent control."

"And the rat was Barry Stiles," I said.

"He recognized me. He threatened to expose me if I didn't fire Kuchen." He gave a short raspy laugh. "Can't have rats in a restaurant."

He aimed the gun at me.

"Why 'almost perfect'?" I said to keep him talking.

"What?"

"You said I was 'almost perfect' for your purposes. Why almost?"

"I knew you had been an accountant. That worried me a little, but I figured all you were going to do was make chargers. I had no idea the staff would cook up this hare-brained idea of an Austrian/Fusion restaurant and even less that you would get involved."

"Why did you let them go through with it?"

He shrugged. "I guess it won't hurt to tell you at this point. As you saw in the meeting, I was opposed to it at first. But I was thinking while that idiot Billot was talking. I figured if I refused to let them try, they might attempt to track down the investors and get them to approve the plan. The staff seemed determined, and I didn't want them snooping around. But the best reason for me to let then go forward was I thought they would make the failure story even more complete. I still can't believe those idiots are making money."

"So when they started turning a profit, you tried to undermine them by making an anonymous call to the police telling them to check Barry Stiles' body for barium carbonate."

"Yeah, that was me. What else?" he asked.

"You got Wallace Voile to picket."

His eyes narrowed. "You know too much."

"I know you swindled the investors," I admitted, "but I have no interest in that. I just want to get out of here and forget the whole nightmare."

"If you're not interested in the swindle, why were you poking around in my office?" He waved the gun at me. "And don't tell me any crap about a burglar being here before you arrived."

"Okay," I said, "here's the truth. I was trying to get into the safe to get back my five thousand dollars." I told him about the advance I had made to pay the staff the morning after the Grand Re-opening. Or Second Opening. Or Second Coming. By whichever name, I wished it had never happened.

"Forget the five thousand dollars," I said. "Use it to fix the window I cut. Just let me walk away. I'll never say anything about the swindle."

An evil grin curled his lips. "You're forgetting about Barry Stiles."

"What's that got to do with anything?" I bluffed. "I barely knew him."

"Which is why the cops let you go. That and the fact they think Dorfmeister did it."

I shrugged. "Maybe he did." I felt like a rat saying it, but my life was on the line, and I could always apologize to Jürgen later. Unless he turned out to be the accomplice.

A light seemed to go on in Molinero's eyes. "What the police need is stronger evidence. Like a confession. And you're going to write one. Pick up that pen."

"I didn't kill him," I shouted.

He was manic now, his face pulsing through a rainbow of orange and red shades. "I know that, but the police don't. Write, 'I killed Barry Stiles' and sign it."

"There's nothing to write on."

"Use the desk blotter, you shrimp."

"Don't you think the police will wonder why I broke into your dead-bolted office to write a confession? Maybe they'll figure out you forced me to do it."

"Write it on a piece of paper. I can plant it somewhere else." I started to open the top right-hand drawer.

"No tricks," he said. "Open the drawer on your left."

He said he knew a lot about me, but he obviously didn't know I'm left-handed.

The drawer on the left was just under the plastic tub of jalapeño juice. My heart was pounding and my hand shaking, but I managed in one continuous motion to grab the jug and sling its contents in his face. The jalapeño juice wasn't useless after all.

Molinero yelped and bent over in pain when the stinging liquid hit his eyes. I raced around the desk before he could regain his composure and pushed him to the ground. I flung the door aside and ran headlong into the chair I had placed on the kitchen side of the door.

Which was a good thing because that was probably why the bullet that whizzed by missed me. I rolled to the side to escape Molinero's line of fire. But when I started to get up, I saw M'Lanta Scruggs running at me with a pistol in his hand.

The first thought that ran through my mind was I was right about him being the accomplice. He had been first on my list because of his being able to get into Molinero's office.

My second thought was *I am about to die.*

He raised the pistol. I closed my eyes. Another bullet whizzed by. I heard a scream from behind me and then a thump. I opened my eyes and turned to see Santiago Molinero sprawled on the floor, his gun in his hand. His ochre face had streaks and blotches the color of normal Caucasian skin.

Shaking uncontrollably, I turned back to see Scruggs walking calmly towards me, gun in hand. There was nothing I could do. Even if there had been, I was too scared to do it. He stood over me like a black Goliath. He opened his jacket and returned the gun to a shoulder holster. Then he reached into his coat's inner pocket and pulled out a leather folder. He extended it down with his long arm and flipped it open to reveal an impressive shield.

"Charles Webbe," he said, "Federal Bureau of Investigation."

56

I held my glass up to the light. "*Nopalitos*," I said

"What about them?" asked Susannah.

"I just realized it. The margaritas here are the same shade of green as *nopalitos*."

She lofted her glass. "You're right."

Angie materialized next to us. "You two wanting a refill?"

"Just admiring the color," I said.

"But since you're here," said Susannah, and Angie smiled and left to get refills.

"So what was the big break-through you were about to explain?" Susannah asked.

"I was sitting in court while a senile-looking judge, Layton and a woman named Rincon from the D.A.'s office discussed my future. The longer they talked, the more nervous I became. I felt so . . . helpless. It was my future, but I had no say in it. I was a piece of driftwood on the river, a cog in a wheel. I was being ground by the wheels of justice, I—"

"Cut the metaphors, Hubie, and get to the point."

"Right. I was in a mill. 'Mill'—that was the key word. I thought of the *Moulin Rouge* because *moulin* means mill in French. Then I realized it's a cognate with the Spanish word for mill, *molina*." I looked at her. "That's not as common as you might suspect. French and Spanish are both romance languages, but they don't share—"

"Hubert, I've got class tonight. Can you get to the point? I won't be able to concentrate if you leave me hanging about this mystery."

"Sorry. So *molina* took me to *molinero*, the Spanish word for the person who operates a mill."

"A miller."

"Right. Then I remembered Rafael listing all the people he remembered from Café Alsace." I did a little drum roll on the table. "One of them was Jim Miller, and he was the manager."

She stared at me.

"*Jim*, get it? Short for James. Which in Spanish is *Santiago*."

She stared some more. Then she said, "So Jim Miller and Santiago Molinero had the same name in two different languages? That's the big breakthrough clue?"

"No, they shared more than just a name. They are—were—the same person."

"There must be lots of people named Santiago Molinero and even more named James Miller. That doesn't make them all the same person."

"Of course not. But these two were." I hesitated. "Or this one was? I don't know how to talk about two people being one. Anyway, there were other clues pointing in that direction, but I didn't see them until I thought about the two of them being one."

"Such as?"

"In the order in which I saw them—"

"Or the order in which you missed them," she said. We both laughed just as Angie showed up with our refills.

"I guess you're glad to see me," she said.

After Angie left, I continued my explanation. "It might be a coincidence that there was a James Miller at *Alsace* and a Santiago Molinero at *Schnitzel,* but for them both to be the manager is a double coincidence. That was enough to start me wondering."

She perked up. "You were right to start wondering. The hardest part about an alias is remembering it. You decide to call yourself Frank Smith and then the next day, you introduce yourself to someone as Fred Smith or Frank Jones and blow your cover."

"Really?"

"Sure. It happens all the time."

"How many people have you ever known who adopted an alias?"

"Dozens. In murder mysteries."

Here we go again, I thought.

"So," she elaborated, "what they do is choose something based on their real name. Like Richard Franklin might become Frank Richards."

"And James Jesse might become Jesse James," I added.

She cocked her head to the side. "I didn't know he used an alias."

Neither did I.

"So what was the next step?" she asked.

"His skin was a weird color. At first, I just thought it was odd. But when I started speculating that Molinero might be Miller, I figured it must have been that rub-on instant tanning lotion. Turns out I was right, and guess what?"

"What?"

"Jalapeño juice is a solvent for that stuff. The parts of his face I splashed the jalapeño juice on turned back to his normal skin color. It was weird looking at his face there on the floor—"

"I don't need to know what he looked like dead. Maybe he just wanted that outdoorsy look a tan gives you."

"But he also had a beard."

"Lots of people have beards. And lots of people with Hispanic last names have light skin, so he didn't need to color his skin to appear Hispanic."

"But he wasn't trying just to look Hispanic. He was also trying to look *different*. He needed not to resemble his former self because he knew some people who applied for jobs at *Schnitzel* might be from Café Alsace or one of the other places he's started."

"There were others?"

"*Schnitzel* was his sixth restaurant, all colossal failures."

She shook her head in amazement. "I don't get it. Why would someone who failed so often keep . . . Oh my God! He *wanted* to fail. It's like that movie, *The Producers*, where the accountant teams up with a Broadway producer to deliberately produce a flop. They raise more money than they spend, so when the play closes, they pocket the surplus. The investors figure everything is gone and don't even pursue it."

"Exactly. And remember the name of the musical they produced?"

"Who could forget it? *Springtime for Hitler*. But audiences decided it was a spoof, and the play became a hit."

"So no failure and no unspent money to pocket. See a parallel here?"

She slapped the table and laughed. "*Schnitzel* was the restaurant equivalent of *Springtime for Hitler*, a restaurant doomed to failure."

"Exactly."

"But it became *Chile Schnitzel* and began to succeed like *Springtime for Hitler*. So he had to undermine the restaurant. Let me guess, he's the one who called the police about the poison being your glazing chemical."

"Right."

"And he somehow got Voile to take the wait staff out on strike."

"Right."

"And then he sicced the D.A. on you for larceny."

"He must have, although he didn't admit that one because I didn't ask him about it before the shooting started."

She brightened. "And I'll bet he told Voile to flirt with Rafael so he wouldn't be thinking about Molinero and possibly recognize him."

"I hadn't thought of that one."

"That's because you date two women at once."

"I don't date . . ." I saw she was laughing and cut short my reply.

"Anything else that made you suspicious of Molinero?"

"Yeah, when I took him the glazed sample and the drawing of the edelweiss overlay, he approved them with barely a glance."

She was seeing it all now. "He had insisted that you had to do the work in the restaurant. You thought it was because he wanted oversight and control."

"Right."

"But what he really wanted was for the glazing chemicals to be there in case he needed to poison someone."

"He said it's important to have rodent control in a restaurant."

She shuddered. "Any other clues that Miller and Molinero were the same guy?"

"No, but there was one that should have made me realize he probably wasn't Hispanic. Remember me telling you that during the meeting about restarting the restaurant, Molinero stopped opposing the idea and ask for a show of hands of those in support of the fusion idea?"

"Yeah, but why did he do that? He must have known the vote would be in favor."

"Of course. But he thought *Chile Schnitzel* would be an even bigger failure than *Schnitzel*. He thought we were unwittingly advancing his scheme. So he allowed the vote and appeared very magnanimous in doing so. But when he called the vote, Juan asked him to repeat it in Spanish for the benefit of the staff who didn't speak English. So Molinero said, '*Si les gusta este nuevo plan, levanten los manos*.'"

"So?"

"He said it incorrectly. It should be *las manos*, not *los manos*."

"I thought Spanish words ending in 'o' were always masculine."

"Almost always. But *mano* is one of the few exceptions." I raised my eyebrows in anticipation.

She eyed me warily. "Okay, I'll bite. Why is *mano* an exception?"

"Because *mano* is derived from the Latin *manus* which was a fourth declension feminine noun."

She rolled her eyes. "Four years of Latin and all you got from it is a chance to show off once in a while."

"Not true. Father Groas and I occasionally exchange Roman greetings."

57

Charles Webbe showed up at *Spirits in Clay* promptly at ten as we had agreed. He wore a dark blue suit, a starched white shirt and a regimental tie. His black shoes were polished to a gloss.

So was his head. He had sheared the dreadlocks and shaved what remained, including the beard. I led him to my kitchen where he accepted my offer of fresh coffee. I had put away my usual cheap brand in favor of New Mexico Piñon Coffee.

"How do you take it?"

"Black," he said. "Like your girlfriend."

We both laughed. I offered him a *cuerno de azucar*. He managed to eat it without a single grain of sugar flecking his clothes.

I looked him in the eye, something that was harder to do than it should have been.

"You saved my life."

He shrugged. "It's what we do. The Director gets out of sorts when we lose a civilian."

"I owe you an apology. I thought you were going to shoot me."

"No need to apologize. I generally have the same feeling when someone is running at me with a gun."

"But I thought you were Molinero's accomplice."

"Because you saw me in his office."

I was flabbergasted. "How did you know I saw you?"

"Because I also saw you," he said as if it were obvious.

"But the place was dark, and you never looked at me."

He smiled. "I'm a trained observer. I don't need to look at you to see you."

I felt silly and embarrassed about hiding behind my work table now that I knew he knew I was there all along.

"I saw someone else in the restaurant late one night." I hated to rat on Arliss, but I figured Webbe needed to know.

"Arliss Mansfield," he said.

Sees all, knows all, I thought. "What was he doing there?"

He told me. I felt gloomy.

"How did you get in Molinero's office, anyway?"

He gave me a cold stare. "If I told you, I'd have to kill you." Then he laughed. He had an easy laugh.

"Why didn't you say something when you saw me?"

"I didn't want to blow my cover. Anyway, I figured you'd think I was trying to steal something, and that was fine. Just as long as you didn't know I was looking for evidence."

I nodded.

He smiled broadly. "You probably felt bad about labeling a black man a thief."

"I did."

"Well, don't be too hard on yourself. If I see someone in an office in a closed and dark building, I assume he's a burglar. The color of his skin doesn't matter."

I refilled his cup and he accepted another *cuerno de azucar*.

"So Arliss wasn't the accomplice and neither were you. Can you tell me who it was?"

"Bonnie Miller, but you know her as Wallace Voile."

"So Wallace was an alias. And . . . Wait, Miller? As in James Miller? Macklin Masoot told me she was Molinero's paramour, but I didn't believe him."

"You were right not to believe him."

"She wasn't his paramour?"

He shook his head. "Jim Miller wasn't her lover. He was her father."

I drank some coffee while that sunk in. I had disliked her from the moment we met, but now I saw her not as the icy beauty but as the girl whose father had been killed.

"Why did you pose as a dishwasher?"

"I couldn't pose as a chef. I can't cook. And a black man applying for a dishwashing job doesn't raise anyone's suspicion."

"That's a sad commentary."

"Won't always be that way," he said. His tone reflected both realism and confidence. Maybe those are the ingredients of wisdom, I thought.

"How'd you come up with the name M'Lanta?"

He laughed. "You like it?"

"Not really. But I guess it worked."

"I was trying to find a name when I saw a bottle of the stuff, and I liked the absurdity of it so much, I couldn't resist."

"When I told a friend of mine your name was M'Lanta, she said, 'No wonder he's a potscrubber'. I told her some people might consider that a racist remark."

"Some might. Not me. It's a classist remark. A black man named

R'nandle is at a disadvantage in life. But so is a white man named Jethro. It's harder for the black man because he already has a steeper hill to climb, but names do make a difference."

"R'nandle?"

"Just made it up. Maybe I should have used that rather than M'Lanta."

"Charles Webbe has a nice ring to it," I said.

"It was the name of the best man I ever knew," he said, "my father."

And the name of the man who saved my life, I thought to myself.

58

Susannah said, "I can't believe you tried to crack the safe."

I shook my head at my own folly. "If I'd had the sense not to try, I would've been out of there before Molinero showed up. I wouldn't have been shot at and almost killed."

"What I don't understand is why you went there to begin with. Why not just tell the police your suspicion about Molinero and let them handle it?"

"I thought about doing that. I *wanted* to do that. Skulking around empty buildings goes against my nature. But I kept thinking about that saying that the wheels of justice grind slowly."

"Everyone knows that, Hubie. As sayings go, it's just run of the mill."

"Hey, I'm the one who makes puns," I complained after I laughed.

"Yeah, but sometimes a girl needs revenge."

"I knew if I turned it over to the police, it would eventually work out. But in the meantime, someone else might get killed."

"Because someone else might recognize Miller and become a threat to him like Barry did?"

"Right. Or he might try to kill Alain or another worker to put *Chile Schnitzel* out of business."

"So you decided to play hero and do it yourself."

"You know I lack the hero gene. All I had to do was find a second set of books and take them away. I didn't think it would be dangerous."

"But you *made* it dangerous. You prolonged your stay by carefully cutting out the window and then trying to crack the safe. Why not just smash the window, rifle through the desk and be gone?"

"A guy could get hurt with broken glass flying everywhere. And I don't like making a mess."

"Jeez."

The little pun devil spoke to me. "Besides, my solution was paneless."

"Double jeez. Why did you think Molinero had an accomplice?"

"I just thought that dragging a dead body through a parking garage and hoisting it into the back of my Bronco was too much for one person. Even if Molinero could lift the body, he'd need a lookout at the very least. And Scruggs seemed the likeliest accomplice because I had seen him in Molinero's office."

"You also saw Arliss in the restaurant late at night."

"And I put him on the list of possible accomplices, but it turns out he was there for another reason."

"Which was?"

I sighed. "He was taking food."

"Arliss Mansfield is a thief?"

"It wasn't like Escoffier. He wasn't sending it to a second family or selling it for profit. The poor guy is broke. He didn't even have enough money to buy food. So he took some."

"Why didn't he just ask?"

"Probably too proud. Maybe he planned to reimburse the restaurant once he got paid. I don't know what he was thinking."

"So it wasn't Scruggs—Webbe—and it wasn't Arliss. Who was it?"

"You picked Wallace Voile as the murderess. You almost had it. She was the accomplice."

"I knew she was *something*," she said excitedly. "The first clue was using an alias. I was right, wasn't I? Wallace is an alias."

"Yes. And so is Voile."

"What's her real name?"

"Bonnie Miller."

She inhaled audibly. "Miller's wife?"

"His daughter."

"God. Now I feel awful."

We sat in silence for a while.

"Tell me something happy," said Susannah.

"M'Lanta Scruggs cleaned up well."

"He looked like a thug," she said. "I was kind of afraid of him."

"You should have seen him this morning. He was immaculate in a business suit, white shirt and rep tie. His head was shaved and shiny, like a bowling ball."

"That's not a politically correct thing to say, Hubert."

"You're right. Bowling balls come in all sorts of colors now. I should have said, 'a *black* bowling ball'."

She shook her head and signaled for Angie.

I took a sip of the fresh margarita just to make sure it was as good as the first one. It was.

"I'll tell you something else happy. Trying to crack that safe made me think of the famous safe cracker, Jimmy Valentine. As fate would have it, he fell in love with the daughter of a banker. The banker had some sort of reception at the bank one night and Valentine was invited. Two young girls were playing near the safe. One of them ran into the safe and the other one playfully pushed the door shut. But it had a time-lock and would not open for twenty four hours. By then, the little girl would have suffocated. There was panic among the guests, especially the mother of the little girl in the safe. Valentine stepped to the safe and turned the tumblers. He felt the clicks that revealed the combination because he sandpapered his fingers to make them sensitive. He opened the safe and the child was saved."

"That's a nice story."

"Wait. It gets better. A policeman was among the attendees at the party. When he saw the man open the safe, he knew it must be Jimmy Valentine. Valentine recognized the policemen. Knowing he had blown his cover, he walked up to the officer and held out his hands for the cuffs, saying, 'You saw it all. Now you must do your duty.' But the detective said, 'I thought you were someone I'm after, but I see I was mistaken. You are a better man than the one I seek'. M'Lanta Scruggs seemed to be a potscrubber with attitude, but he, too, was a better man than I realized."

"Is that really a true story?"

I smiled at her. "Sure. He saved my life."

She rolled her eyes. "The story about Jimmy Valentine. Is that true?"

"I doubt it. It was written by William Sydney Porter, another person who used an alias."

"What was his alias?"

"O. Henry."

59

I made my final trip to Santa Fe the next morning to meet with a forensic accountant from the FBI.

When he suggested we work in Molinero's office, I told him there was no way I was going into the kitchen, much less the office. I was adamant about not returning to the scene of the shoot out.

We sat in my previous work space—the private dining room—and went through the documents.

What a mess. Unpaid invoices included the heavy wood entry doors, the clay and glazing supplies and a ticket for Kuchen from Albuquerque back to Vienna. There was a change of planes in New York, of course. Most of the flights from Albuquerque's Sunport are provided by Southwest Airlines. I don't think they fly to Vienna.

I turned over all my records and explained what I knew about the operations of *Schnitzel* and *Chile Schnitzel*. As I walked away, it felt like those records must have weighed a hundred pounds. But when I reached the door, I couldn't leave.

I remembered that first day when the staff had performed their pantomime for Kuchen. I pictured Juan the bacon chopper whose family name I never knew, Barry and Santiago—or Jim—both dead. I thought of Arliss, Jürgen, Helen, Alain, Machlin, Maria and Raoul, out of work. I wondered if Bonnie was headed for prison. It was a bizarre chapter of my life. I needed to turn the page.

I walked to Maria's apartment.

"Hubie, I'm surprised to see you here." She smiled as she stood in the doorway, but she did not invite me in.

"I'm surprised to be here," I responded. "I had to meet with someone from the FBI, so I figured as long as I was in Santa Fe—"

"You'd stop by for a nap on my love seat?" Our laughter was hollow.

"No, just to apologize."

"No apology necessary."

I didn't know what else to say. Then a voice I recognized said from inside the apartment, "You're letting all the heat out."

"Guess I better get back inside."

"Goodbye, Maria."

"Bye, Hubie"

60

I went by feats of Clay on my way home to cancel the plate project only to find they had completed it.

I came home with a hundred plates, each sporting my red and green chile design. After explaining my predicament, they had agreed to charge me only ten dollars a plate for the firing. Of course the clay and glazing material had never been paid for, but the FBI would have to sort out the finances of *Schnitzel* and Santiago Molinero/James Miller.

I opened for business and put one of the plates on the counter. I went to the kitchen and started stacking the other ninety-nine plates under my sink next to the Ajax and the Windex. The bong signaled the arrival of a customer. I continued stacking, figuring the customer would browse.

A combination of weariness with stacking and concern about shoplifting eventually drove me to the front. The customer was holding the plate. "How much is this?" she asked.

"One hundred dollars," I said. "And it's handmade."

"By you?"

"I designed it. Someone else fired it."

"Would you sign it for me?"

"Sure."

While she signed a check, I signed the bottom of the plate with an Axner overglaze pen.

"You can have the plate fired again if you want the signature to become part of the glaze."

"I just plan to keep my fresh chilies on it. And maybe use it as a centerpiece from time to time. Will the signature last without firing if I use it that way?"

I told her it would and wrapped the plate.

I chuckled when she left, recalling my words to Molinero: "I'm like the artisans I represent," I had told him, "I do only traditional work."

If I had stuck to my principles, the nightmare at *Schnitzel* never would have happened. Maybe there was a lesson there. I called Dolly and invited her for dinner.

The sale of a second plate shortly before closing buoyed my spirits. If I eventually sold all one hundred, I'd gross ten thousand dollars. I had paid a thousand for the glazing, so I would net nine thousand. I could use four thousand to pay off my hotel bill, and still have five thousand left over to use for . . . what?

The Barry Stiles Scholarship Fund for someone from Martin's pueblo who wanted to attend culinary school.

61

Martin and I showed up at *Dos Hermanas* to find Susannah already there. Two margaritas and a Tecate were waiting.

Well, one margarita was waiting. The other one had started without us. Susannah was not her bubbly self.

"Rafael called me today and cancelled the date we had tonight. I didn't take it well, guys."

"You say something you regret?" asked Martin.

"It was the third time he's cancelled on me. What I said to him was, 'Don't bother calling again.' It felt good at the time, but now I'm beginning to regret it."

"Don't," I said.

"Why?"

"I went by Maria's apartment today to apologize."

"And you regret it?"

"No, I needed to do it. But while I was standing on her porch, I heard a man's voice coming from inside the apartment."

She put her elbow on the table and her chin in her hand. She looked at Martin and then back at me.

"Rafael?"

I nodded.

She lifted her chin off her hand and exhaled. She took a big swig of her drink. "I'm getting better at this," she said.

Neither Martin nor I said anything.

"I used to rush in, fall too hard, but I guess I've become more wary. I wish girls didn't have to be wary. That would be a better world."

Martin and I continued to remain silent.

"There was a lot to like about Rafael," she said. "He's handsome and has a good sense of humor. But there was something else."

"The way he looked at other girls?" I asked.

"You noticed that, too?"

"Sort of obvious."

"Well, it's no big deal. We only had three dates. It's not like I was in love with him. But still . . ."

"You want a hug?" Martin asked.

She nodded, and he stood up and opened his arms. She stepped into them and he embraced her.

When she sat back down, he looked at me. "How about you, *kemo sabe?*"

Susannah laughing was contagious. The three of us must have laughed for a full minute.

"So what about you, Hubie?" she asked. "Are you sorry you fell asleep on Maria's loveseat?"

"I was the next morning, but now that I see how things have worked out, it was probably for the best. I don't need to complicate my life. I'm happy with Dolly. We'll see how things go."

"What about you, Martin? You going to stay a bachelor like Hubie?"

"Diogenes said, 'A man who takes a wife and children gives hostages to fate'."

"That is *so* pessimistic," said Susannah.

"I guess that's why they call him a cynic," said Martin.

That started another laughing jag.

Susannah suggested we have another round.

While we waited, Susannah said, "Isn't this a peachy way to spend a Saturday night? A girl who can't get a guy, a guy who doesn't want a girl, and a guy who has one but doesn't know if he wants to trade her in. Sitting in a tortilla factory drinking margaritas."

"And a Tecate," added Martin.

"Sounds like my definition of a fun time," I said.

"Can't do this on the Rez," said Martin.

"I guess it's not that bad a way to spend the evening."

"Thanks a lot," Martin and I said in unison.

When our second round came, Susannah lifted her glass. "To the three Musketeers."

Martin and I glanced at each other and said in unison—"*Tous pour un, un pour tous.*"

Acknowledgments

Most of the places mentioned in the Pot Thief books are real. The Gruet Winery, La Placita Restaurant and Treasure House Books in Albuquerque and the La Fonda Hotel, La Casa Sena Restaurant and Collected Works Bookstore in Santa Fe are just a few examples. I include them for veracity and also because they are some of my favorite places. What would life be without fine bookstores, restaurants, hotels and champagne?

Special thanks go to Linda Aycock—excellent proofreader, good friend and wife of my high school buddy and still best friend, Jim.

More thanks for Professor Ofélia Nikolova. She kept é and è straight and handled all the other arcane marks over French words. Kenneth Krivanek teaches German and corrected spellings for the German words, but he is not to blame for my decision not to follow the German practice of capitalizing every noun.

Among the many persons who read advanced copies of this

269

book, I wish to acknowledge Mary Louise Rogers of Las Cruces who went over every line with great care, Lucinda Surber of Santa Fe and Kate Feuille of El Paso.

Special thanks to the late Enid Schantz of Lyons, Colorado for her assistance and support. Enid was a major figure in the mystery fiction field. Authors and readers everywhere were deeply saddened by her death.

As always, I relied heavily on the support and advice of my daughter Claire and my wife Lai.

About the Author

J. Michael Orenduff grew up in a house so close to the Rio Grande that he could Frisbee a tortilla into Mexico from his backyard. While studying for an MA at the University of New Mexico, he worked during the summer as a volunteer teacher at one of the nearby pueblos. After receiving a PhD from Tulane University, he became a professor. He went on to serve as president of New Mexico State University.

Orenduff took early retirement from higher education to write his award-winning Pot Thief murder mysteries, which combine archaeology and philosophy with humor and mystery. Among the author's many accolades are the Lefty Award for best humorous mystery, the Epic Award for best mystery or suspense ebook, and the New Mexico Book Award for best mystery or suspense fiction. His books have been described by the *Baltimore Sun* as "funny at a very high intellectual level" and "deliciously delightful," and by the *El Paso Times* as "the perfect fusion of murder, mayhem and margaritas."

OPEN ROAD
INTEGRATED MEDIA

Open Road Integrated Media is a digital publisher and multimedia content company. Open Road creates connections between authors and their audiences by marketing its ebooks through a new proprietary online platform, which uses premium video content and social media.

CPSIA information can be obtained
at www.ICGtesting.com
Printed in the USA
LVOW12s2346210317
528021LV00001B/52/P